CUPCAKES & CORPSES, CONFESSIONS OF A CLOSET MEDIUM, BOOK 5

A SUPERNATURAL SOUTHERN COZY MYSTERY ABOUT A RELUCTANT GHOST WHISPERER

NYX HALLIWELL

Beach Path Publishing, LLC

Cupcakes & Corpses, Confessions of a Closet Medium

Nyx Halliwell

January 25th, 2022

ISBN: 978-1-948686-51-8

Cover Art by EDH Graphics

Formatting by Beach Path Publishing, LLC

Editing by Elizabeth Neal, Patricia Essex

Please Note

ACKNOWLEDGMENTS

Writing this series is so much fun, and I'm forever grateful for those who've encouraged me to do it. I love to create new characters and worlds based on my own, and Ava is straight from my heart.

Thank you to those who love Mama, Rosie, Tabby, and the rest. Even Winter and Mamma N are dear to me, and I'm thrilled so many of you look forward to their appearances in these stories. (If you want more of them, be sure to check out the Sister Witches of Raven Falls. You'll get more of Persephone in Winter's story, Of Spirits and Superstition, too).

As always, I have the pleasure of bouncing ideas off my Official Reader Group and must thank them for Regan and Brynlee's names. Getting to create these stories with input from my biggest fans is a dream come true.

Lastly, I thank the spirits who inspire these stories, as well. I love writing ghost characters and hope to keep bringing my readers more adventures with them!

ONE

Amockingbird outside the window chirps fervently, as if he'd like me to pour him a cup of coffee as I stand at the sink filling mine. I love how he mimics other birds, going through a lovely repertoire of trills and notes, happy as can be.

Logan comes up behind me and kisses my neck. "Ready for tomorrow?"

My fiancé's breath is warm, tickling the delicate skin, and I grin. I've been doing that a lot lately. "Pinch me. I can't believe it's actually happening."

My cats, Arthur and Lancelot, eat noisily, barely taking time to breathe as they inhale their chow. Moxley, Logan's dog, stands next to them, crunching his kibble with slow, conscientious determination. Tabby, my shape shifting grandmother who spends her days in feline form, eyes me with disdain for the cat food, her narrowed gaze demanding fresh pâté.

Logan turns me so we're face-to-face. "You and Rhys were up late."

Our next door neighbor and friend has been helping prepare for my dream wedding to Logan Cross III. He's been living here for nearly a month, since giving up his place to his brother, Charles. Charles is also engaged, and his fiancée, Trysta, is opening a bakery in Logan's former business.

I try not to think about her and concentrate on the man in front of me. My whirlwind romance with Logan has my head spinning. Feeling like I could burst into song along with the mockingbird, I lose myself in his pretty blue eyes and run my fingers through his wheat-colored hair. I am the luckiest woman on the planet. "We were working on last minute alterations on my veil. I thought it needed a bit of sparkle."

"You make everything sparkle." He returns my smile. "I can't wait to see it."

Arthur and Lancelot finish before Moxley, the two staring at the dog and his bowl with intense concentration. Although the basset hound never leaves a crumb behind, the cats continue their wishful thinking. "I want everything to be perfect."

Logan rubs my arms. "It will be."

Tabby screeches and I flinch. I'm about to chastise her, believing she's complaining about her food service, when Trysta appears in the kitchen doorway. "Perfect for what?"

We both jump, and Tabby hisses. Moxley growls, coming to stand next to Logan. I'm not the only one in this household who doesn't like this gal.

"What are you doing here?" My heart bangs in my chest like thunder. Not only do I not want Trysta here, the wedding is a secret—only a few close friends know about it, along with my parents. Helen Cross, Logan's mother, will string us up if she finds out.

Besides, Trysta is not actually alive, and I have to break her attachment to Logan's brother before she does him serious harm.

I see ghosts, and most of the time, I help those stuck on the earthly plane to pass over. Trysta apparently has no plans to move on, and she's going to be a troublemaker, I can feel it in my bones.

Her energy generally makes my stomach revolt because she has attached herself to three male spirits. They share a weird connection I haven't figured out yet. That bond keeps her in human form. Yes, she's a ghost, but she is able to circumvent it by sucking up the living energy of those men. Having her in my house gives me the creeps, and although I can't see or sense those attached to her, I'm relieved I haven't eaten yet.

She bats her brown eyes at Logan and offers him a tray of cupcakes. Her apron is dotted with flour and the scent of cinnamon wafts to us. "I'm experimenting with a new recipe." Her voice is child-like and overly cheerful. "I know how much you love cinnamon, Logi. You have to try one and tell me what you think."

Vexation ripples through me and my territorial instincts kick in hard. The nickname is bad enough, but she's flirting with him right in front of me. In *my* kitchen, as if I'm not even here. I want to smack the tray from her hands, but I don't want to clean up the mess it would make, nor do I want the dog and cats to eat anything she's baked. "How did you get in?"

Her gaze flicks to me, away. "Through the front door, silly. I figured bringing you breakfast was the least I could do since Logi gave up his place for the bakery."

He reaches for the tray. "It's nothing, really."

I not-so-accidentally elbow him and stay his hand with mine. She's not getting off that easily. "The door is locked."

Her brows dip and she gives me a look suggesting I'm confused. "No, it isn't, honey. I walked right in."

Right through *it, you mean.*

"I love coming over here." She scans the homey kitchen, taking in my aunt's knickknacks, the appliances and table. "It's so snug and cozy. I feel like a huge weight lifts right off my shoulders when I step inside. Being here is...peaceful."

I need to up my game to keep ghosts out. Unwanted ones, anyway. My Aunt Willa and my great-grandfather, Sam, are always welcome. "You should try knocking." I refuse to let this go. Even ghosts need manners. "You don't barge into someone's house *uninvited*."

"We're practically family, Ava." Her tone is chastising. In fact, it rings of Helen Cross. "And people come and go from here daily without knocking. I thought you were open for business already, is all. You don't have to get bristle-y about it. You're so tense all the time. " She slides the tray toward me. "Have a cupcake. It'll make you feel loads better."

The only way I'll feel better is if I can stop her from leaching energy off my future brother-in-law and send her, and her cupcakes, to the other side.

Unfortunately, in the past couple weeks I've been trying to do just that, and it has proven to be harder than expected. She's an unusual ghost with deep hooks in Chuck, and I can't have him end up like the others attached to her.

Silver cords run between them and Trysta. The men are acting as her battery chargers, giving her what she needs to stay corporeal. A black widow ghost, my guardian angel calls her. And if I don't sever her connection to those men, sending her to the afterlife could harm them and Charles.

Logan pats my hand and accepts the tray. "We'll check these out after we've showered." He sets the cupcakes on the table and guides her out. Moxley sticks close—smart dog. "Thanks for bringing them over. Have a good day at the bakery."

I hang back, but keep her in sight. To my surprise, the door is wide open. Logan glances at me as he leads her out.

Trysta stops before the threshold and bounces onto her tip

toes to kiss his cheek. "I'm so excited for the grand opening on Saturday, but I still need to hire more staff. And then there's all the baking!" Her eyes are lit with joy.

He nearly pushes her out to the porch. "You're going to be busy, that's for sure."

"Let me know about the new recipe," she calls as she skips down the steps.

He waves before shutting the door and leaning against it. Moxley, Arthur, and Lancelot climb into the display window and watch her take the sidewalk and swing through the gate near the road. "We have to do something about her, and soon."

I nod, and the freshly brewed coffee once again smells good and I'm in desperate need of some. "Can you believe that? Now she's waltzing in here like she owns the place. Gives me the creeps."

He pushes off and heads my way. "That's saying something, considering you deal with the dead on a regular basis. I thought you had salt or rocks or something to keep spirits out. Whatever you're using, it's not working."

"She's unique, and not in a good way." In the kitchen, I dump the cupcakes in the trash. "The salt and crystals work on the undead. She's not one hundred percent ghost, hence they don't affect her. Sage is researching options, and I don't want to keep out Aunt Willa or Sam, so I haven't used anything stronger, like sigils or spells. This is a tougher spirit problem than I've previously encountered."

A brief longing glance at the trash—he really does love cinnamon—and he kisses my forehead. "How about we have some Beehive food for breakfast?"

I pour us both coffee and hand him a cup. "Wish I could. I have an early client."

"No rest for the wicked," he teases, clinking my mug with his.

"Or the successful," I add. "Trysta isn't the only who needs extra staff."

He leans a hip on the table. "Thought you were interviewing bookkeepers this week."

My strong suit is party planning and designing gowns. It's definitely *not* profit and loss statements or tax spreadsheets. Even the last app I tried was too complicated for my brain. "Mama insists I use Pell Abrams, so I'll have to speak to him to make her happy."

"He's still alive?"

I chuckle. "He's got to be pushing ninety, and I admire his work ethic. I'm sure he's a fine CPA, but I'm leaning toward hiring a gal named Ophelia Chen. It's a work-study program the high school has instituted and she could start this summer and get credit for it. Her counselor tells me she's super smart, is a whiz with numbers, and is eager to learn."

"Sounds like a good option, but are you okay with trusting a kid with your financial reports?"

"From what I understand, she does bookkeeping and inventory for her mom, who runs a hair salon out of their home. She wants to get more experience than just the family business, so she's coming in tomorrow to see if we click. Fingers crossed."

He makes the motion with his. "After I walk Moxley, I'll pick up breakfast. You have to eat."

My phone rings in the other room. "Okay, you twisted my arm." And I'm starving. "Biscuits and eggs for me. I bet Queenie has a cinnamon scone. A better replacement for the cupcakes."

Once he has Moxley on a leash, they leave through the front door. I smile as I watch Logan trying to get the dog to run. The chubby guy gives it a go, but his short legs aren't made for it. Logan cheers him on anyway, and I love the man even more.

Sun streams in through one of the windows, highlighting

the latest wedding dress on display. Logan turns to wave at me once he and Mox have cleared the gate. It's nice to have him living here, using the extra bedroom and an empty downstairs room for his attorney business. We've fallen into an easy rhythm, and I look forward to becoming Mrs. Logan Cross. While butterflies nervously tickle my stomach at the thought, I'm ready.

As he and the dog disappear, my gaze tracks across the street. The building Logan owns has undergone a lot of change in the recent weeks, his law office sign in storage and a Killer Cupcakes sign in its place. Across the front porch hangs a Grand Opening Soon banner.

The irony of the shop name appalls me. With plans for the secret wedding, and everything else on my plate, it's difficult to find time to dig deeper into Trysta's background, but I have to. Another reason I need help with my business and fast.

Movement in the bakery's front window catches my eye. The black widow is staring out, her gaze tracking what I can no longer see.

Logan.

As if she senses me, her attention shifts. I instinctively step back, hoping I'm no longer in the spotlight of the glass. Her face is blank, but her eyes are now as dark as the chocolate she uses in her baking. Those instincts kick in hard once more and I open the door and stare back at her. "Persephone," I say out loud. "I need help."

The gargoyles that decorate the top of the stair landings snicker in unison. "You sure do," one remarks.

The cat door knocker joins in. "And a lot of it."

Yes, I can also hear these inanimate objects speak. They've been here as long as I can remember, and I think Aunt Willa somehow enchanted them.

The angel appears on the porch near the rocking chairs.

Tabby emerges from some unseen shadow and sits at Persephone's feet. The three of us look fixedly at Trysta.

Sam becomes visible, sitting his ghostly form in a chair. "May I join the party?"

Trysta sees us all. She gives a smile, filled with the same darkness as in her eyes, and fades into the shop's shadows.

TWO

Drawing a sigh of relief, I go inside and grab my phone. My local witchy expert, Sage, answers after several rings. "I need to protect Logan," I tell her.

She audibly yawns. "Amulet."

Right. I used a protection necklace at Christmas to ward off an evil spirit. "Will it be enough?"

"Are we talking about the wacko gal across the street?"

"Yes. She's coming into my house uninvited and she's flirting with him."

"Miserable ghost. I hate it when that happens." Another yawn. I'd clearly woken her. "Give me an hour."

I thank her and hang up. Persephone appears to let me know she will follow Logan and make sure Trysta stays away. I jump in the shower and am out before the two of them return.

While Logan doesn't see my guardian angel unless she wants him to, I let him know she might be bopping in and out. I don't mention that his future sister-in-law is the reason, and he assumes it's part of my normal ghost-whispering gig, which it kind of is.

I ask him to wear the necklace, and that makes him suspicious. He eyes it with disdain. "Why?"

"We both need extra protection with Trysta running around." It's the truth. "I'd feel better if I know you wear this."

He doesn't put it around his neck but does drop it in his suit coat pocket. Then he kisses me and leaves to pick up breakfast.

At my desk, I prepare for my first client. My mother's friend, Hannah Grady, has asked for a consult, which I assume is for her upcoming fiftieth birthday. Imagine my surprise when she plunks down in the chair across from mine, her arm in a sling, and tells me in a hushed voice, "I have a...ghost problem."

In general, Mama isn't one to promote my abilities or send folks to me, so I know Hannah must be in real trouble. "I see. Can I offer you a cup of coffee?" I sure need one.

"Oh, no, I'm jittery enough as it is." She glances around as though a ghost might jump out and scare her at any second. "It's unnerving, you know?"

Following her gaze, I scan the room, and then her immediate personal space. Usually, I can detect an earthbound spirit with no problem.

I still see nothing near her. Perhaps my salt and crystals are working to keep him out, or he isn't attached to her specifically, but to her home or an item she owns. "Do you know this ghost?"

She leans forward and whispers, "He's my ex."

Again, I automatically scan the vicinity, expecting to see a phantom man hanging with us. Nothing. "Where have you spotted him?"

"Well, I haven't *seen* him, per se, but he's around. At home, when I'm out in public—I can feel him watching me. I can't sleep, this." She raises her arm.

I zero in on the sling. "How did that happen?"

"The other night I got up to use the bathroom and there

was one of my shoes in the middle of the floor. I never turn on the bathroom light, since I know my way around my own home, and there was plenty of moonlight through the window. But I never expected it to be lying there! I tripped, hit my head on the tub, and pulled a muscle in my shoulder."

"And you think your ex placed it there?"

"I know he did." Her face is stern. "It was one of my old slip-ons. Sly hated those things. Always said they were frumpy. But they're so comfortable, you know?"

I pull out one of my intake forms for brides and write down her name along with a note about the shoe in the comments section at the bottom. While she's friends with Mama, I don't know her or her history. Since I don't have forms for ghost whispering, I want to make sure I get the facts straight. "How and when did Sly die?"

She angles her head to read what I'm writing. "Sylvester died twenty years ago while he was hunting north of here along Cap Cold Ridge. They found his backpack, rifle, and coat. The coat and backpack had been ravaged by an animal, probably a bear or mountain cat. Lots of blood." She visibly shivers. "They never found his body, even though they searched for weeks. The medical examiner claimed he couldn't have survived, based on the amount of blood loss, and they assumed the animal dragged him off to a den and... Well, you get the picture."

Unfortunately, I do. "Why do you think he's haunting you now?"

She turns the palm of her uninjured hand up. "I don't know. Because I'm getting married again?"

That could do it. "Congratulations." I don't see an engagement ring, but maybe she doesn't want one. "After twenty years. That's a long time."

"Yes. I've had serious relationships since, but things didn't work out."

"Sly never bothered you over those?" She shakes her head. So what is it about this current one that upsets the spirit? "When he was alive, did Sly know your fiancé?"

She gnaws her bottom lip. "Burt is his former best friend."

Bingo. "And were you two…"—I try to be delicate with the suggestion, in case I'm off base—"involved while you and Sly were together? I'm not prying out of curiosity; it just helps me get a feel for why he's doing it after all this time. I need to figure out his motive."

A blush turns her already pink cheeks pinker. "Oh, no. Burt was always kind to me back then, but… We reconnected a few months ago, after he lost his wife."

"I see." I scribble down his name and the information. "So Sly is haunting your house, correct?" I still could see nothing attached to her spirit-wise, and wished Persephone was here to confirm he wasn't lurking somewhere. On the other hand, if my preventative factors were keeping him out, hooray. I just wished they'd work on Trysta.

"My car, too. It's been acting up and I've never had issues with it before."

That is serious. We can't risk her ending up in an accident while driving. I get to my feet. "Let me get something from upstairs and I'll be right back."

I search through my aunt's trunk and find the items I want. Returning to Hannah, I light the sage bundle, hand her a black kyanite crystal, and ask Sylvester to step forward and show himself.

Nothing happens except that the bundle doesn't go out, and smoke fills the downstairs. Arthur and Lancelot, who've been lounging in their favorite spot in the display window, jet to the second floor. Moxley whines and disappears as well.

Coughing and apologizing, I open the front door and toss the smudge bundle outside. Tabby runs out, and Sam laughs from his seat in the rocking chair. He's still there and salutes me. "Would you like me to keep an eye on her for you?"

"Bless you," I say quietly. "I'll do a more formal clearing of her vehicle and home as soon as I can. In the meantime, see if you can pick up on Sly and let me know what you find out about him. I can't see or hear him, but it may be that he couldn't follow her inside."

One long finger strokes his partial beard. "Hmm. I do love a good mystery. Perhaps I'll ask that Sherlock fellow to assist me."

Sherlock is another ghost I deal with on a regular basis. He's fond of Persephone, believes he's the real Sherlock of literary fame, and has helped me with uncooperative spirits in the past. I haven't seen him lately, and wonder if he and my angel are fighting again.

At least this will keep my grandfather busy and help me keep track of Hannah. I return to the foyer, another idea surfacing. "Do you still live in the same home you shared with Sylvester?"

Standing, she gathers her purse and hustles to the door, breathing in fresh air. "It's my family home. My parents passed when I was eighteen and I married Sly a year later. He moved in."

"And when did he move out?"

"He didn't."

"Sorry." The June morning was growing warmer and heat slid up my back. "You divorced him but he didn't move out?"

She fiddles with the crystal. "He didn't sign the papers before he was killed."

"You said he was your ex."

"I consider him to be so. I had the papers, but I didn't find the right time to show them to him. He was a...difficult man to confront."

I shift both of us aside and close the door. People are out and about, and although I don't believe it possible for any of them to hear us, I want her to feel safe sharing her story. "Was he violent toward you?"

Her gaze drops. "He drank. His job with the railroad put a tremendous amount of pressure on him, and he started gambling. He went through our savings, took out credit cards I didn't know about in my name, and when the stress of the job was too much..." I wait, holding my breath, and she confirms it. "He sometimes hit me."

My hackles rise. A violent man in life and still so in death. One way or another, I'm going to send this ghost packing. Hannah deserves her new love and a big dose of happiness. "I will take care of this. Keep the crystal on you at all times. It will help keep him away. I have a full schedule today, but I'll come to your house tonight and see if I can get him to cross over."

"Tonight is book club. You'll be there, right? Your mother said she was bringing you."

I forgot again. "I think your safety is more important."

Pocketing the crystal, she pats my arm. "I'll be careful until then, and we can return to my place after the meeting. I don't want to disappoint your mother."

Mama does tend to put the fear of Dixie Fantome in everyone, even her friends. "If you promise not to take any chances."

A smile softens her lips. "You're a good person, Ava, and I appreciate this."

I move aside to let her out. "Please be careful, okay?"

She stops on the porch and shields her eyes from the sun. "Did you read the book? I loved it. Such a tragic ending, though."

I can't even remember the name of the bestseller Mama and Baylor, our librarian, have chosen for this inaugural get-together. No one needs to know that, though. "Yes, wasn't it a great story?"

I wave as she gets to the gate and both she and Sam wave back. He deftly slips into the passenger seat, her totally unaware. No other ghost is visible.

Logan is exiting his car and carries two white bags stamped with *The Beehive* on the side. At the kitchen table, we unpack our goodies and I chug coffee. The biscuits are still warm and the butter pats have pooled in their centers.

"Did Hannah hire you for her wedding?" Logan asks around a mouthful of his pancakes. Queenie has added a container of fried apples with a generous dash of cinnamon on them.

"I didn't even offer my services for that. She's got a ghost problem, actually."

"Oh, good, because you need another one of those."

"Better get used to it, Cross. My life is filled with them."

"To my beautiful future wife, the ghost-whisperer." He raises his cup. "Our life together will never be dull, that's for sure."

I clink my cup against his and Persephone snorts from the living room. I can't see her, but her presence is reassuring.

The front door opens and Rosie waddles in, her giant pregnant belly appearing before the rest of her. "We have a problem," she calls out.

I suck down another mouthful of eggs, before giving Logan a quick kiss, and taking my coffee with me. Life is never dull with weddings either. "What is it now? Did Lori change her date again? Is Jenn not coming back from maternity leave this week?"

At her desk, she lifts Fern, her Chihuahua, out of her tote bag and tucks it away. The dog lands on a plush bed at her feet. "Gloria's sick. She can't get the final alterations on your dress done by tomorrow."

THREE

In the overall scope of things, not having my dream dress ready for my secret wedding pales to, say, not getting married at all. Or having a deadly ghost after my intended. I'm also worried about my friend. "Is she okay?"

"Said she ate something that didn't agree with her." Rosie angles herself into her chair. She's recently cut her hair to shoulder length, and today has both sides pulled back with combs. Her belly is covered with a bright pink and yellow top, and she's wearing matching pink lipstick. "She went to the clinic where Doc took one look at her and sent her to the hospital. He thinks it's food poisoning."

"Ach." My stomach hurts for her. Had to be serious if Doc wouldn't treat her at our small town clinic. "Poor Gloria."

Logan joins us. "Do they know from what?"

Rosie nods at me and shrugs at Logan. "Not from what she told me this morning."

"Why didn't she call me?" I ask, perplexed.

Rosie wakes up her computer and lifts her paperweight to

snag today's to-do list. "Because you're busy and under tremendous pressure over the wedding. She wanted me to get Rhys to fix the dress without telling you. However,"—she holds up a single finger, swollen slightly but well-manicured—"there's enough secrecy with this whole shenanigan already and I won't be responsible for any of it. I know it's your dream gown, but you'll just have to wear something else. Save it for your real ceremony."

The farther along Rosie gets in her pregnancy, the more short-tempered she's become. Talk about stress, she has way more than I do, and I remind myself to exercise patience. "Okay." I take a deep breath and another gulp of coffee, realizing I need a refill. I've tweaked the pattern and layout of my gown to perfection, but I was working with a prototype. The design had originally come from my teenage mind, and over the years, it has undergone plenty of revisions. The current is as close to my ideal as I can come. "It was only a few seams that needed adjustment. I'm sure Rhys and I can finish it."

Logan's phone rings and he fishes it out. "Gotta take this," he says, reading the screen. "It's Judge Barlow."

Barlow is handling our marriage license. While normally, it would be impossible to keep word about it quiet from that alone, the judge owes Logan a favor and has promised to "lose" the paperwork until Helen's big event in October.

When Logan disappears, I plunk into the chair across from my office manager. She won't look me in the eye. "I apologize for putting you in an uncomfortable position," I tell her.

A palm rests on her belly and she lays her pen down. "Ava, I love that you and Logan want to do things your way and make his mother happy, as well. I applaud your ingenuity and, normally? I'd be the first to encourage your revolt against Helen's controlling, helicopter-parenting, and help you plan it."

"But?"

A heavy sigh and she sinks deeper into her chair. "You're starting a war. I'm not a fan of hers, believe me, but she's a mother. Going behind her back like this is going to create bad juju. Do you really want to start your life with Logan like this? She *will* find out, and she'll never trust you again."

Logan and I have had this discussion several times. On one hand, we want his mother to have her dream ceremony for him. On the other, Logan and I don't want to wait until October to make things official, and my desire to get married in the backyard, surrounded by Aunt Willa's roses and jasmine has been my dream since I started designing dresses. The only conceivable option where Helen and I can both get what we want is having two weddings. Unfortunately, she won't see it that way. It's her way or the highway. "I don't care for it, either, but I don't know how to make all of us happy at the same time. Should I give up my dream for her?"

"You and Logan are adults. You don't need her permission. What you do need is her respect, Ava."

"Hard to earn that when she sees me as being beneath her, no matter what I do."

"I'm not suggesting you make yourself miserable, but being honest with her, even if she does lose her cool, is better than deceiving her." She fiddles with one of her hair combs. "Besides, you've managed to win over some pretty hardcore folks who don't like the fact you see ghosts. On that note, you did Helen a solid at Christmas by saving Logan from their family curse. I think she likes you more than she lets on, and *does* respect you, if begrudgingly. Don't tarnish how far you've come by marrying Logan behind her back."

The front door opens and Sage rambles in, heat and humidity trailing after her. Dressed in a gypsy skirt and tank top, she has a new messenger bag decorated with owls slung over one shoulder and sunglasses covering her eyes. She and her sisters run the Chicks With Gifts Emporium a town over, and have quite a repertoire of witchy and New Age items for sale. As she passes us, she drops a cloth bag into my lap and heads to the kitchen without so much as a hello.

I hear the refrigerator open and close, the clink of ice in a glass, and the fizz of a soda being poured. "Are you going to finish the biscuits?" she calls.

Rosie smiles when I glance at her and gives me a look that says, *kids these days.* Then she hooks her thumb toward Sage. "Did something woo-woo happen I should know about?"

"Tell you later." I get up and take the bag and cup with me. "Good morning to you, too, sunshine. Help yourself." I hold up her gift and examine it. "What's this?"

She grabs a fork from the drawer and drops into my chair at the table. "To help keep out unauthorized houseguests."

Inside are several small items that resemble cameras, some dried herbs, and... "A teddy bear?"

The silverware hits the plate and she gives me a sullen look, removing her glasses. "All that stuff appears normal, but I've placed spells on everything. I want this ghost on video if she enters again without permission. You said she's corporeal. If nothing else, we report her to the cops for trespassing."

It isn't a bad idea. I could just hear her excuses though, and imagine Helen's response if I get Trysta in trouble. "I don't know..."

"If she sees the cameras, and I plan to make sure she does, she'll be mindful of trying to get inside. These aren't simply regular security cameras, they also capture specters. I need to figure out if she's possessing someone or has reanimated her own body."

"Either way, you think showing that to the police will

keep her out? Jones will laugh at a ghost caught on camera." Detective Landon Jones and I aren't exactly friends, and he's usually more than annoyed with any help I provide solving cases. "He'll cheer her on, even if I convince him she is a ghost."

She chews a mouthful and swigs soda. "Take it to your dad. He can get a restraining order against the woman."

Again, it isn't a terrible idea, but it doesn't cover all the ways I need protection from this spirit. "What about Logan? She's definitely eyeing him for some nefarious purpose."

Sage stops chewing. "Nefarious? Have you been doing crossword puzzles again?"

"How do I keep her from getting her claws in him?"

"He's wearing the necklace, right?"

Sort of. "Are you sure it will work against someone like her?"

She shrugs. "I don't have experience with black widows, but it should."

Should seemed like the strongest guarantee I could get for the moment.

"You know, we can perform a cord cutting." She's extended this offer previously. "We can cleave those connections between Trysta and her battery chargers."

"You said that would leave roots, which doesn't solve the problem, because you also mentioned they can grow back."

"It could give you time to figure out your next step. You might get her to cross over, or perhaps those ghosts she's connected to will cross."

"I'm afraid of what that might do to Charles, though, since she already has her hooks in him."

Sage continues eating and though she makes no outward appearance of it, I suspect she's frustrated with me.

I roll one of the bundles of herbs over and flecks of rosemary fall off. "We've already sprinkled this stuff around the foundation. How is this different?"

Finishing my eggs, she wipes her mouth. "My spell is different, and that's a necessary ingredient. I'll make sure Trysta sees me perform that, too. If she knows what's good for her, and I suspect she does, she won't touch your home."

"And the bear?"

"There's a camera inside. It also has an EMF meter that records spikes and spiritual activity. If she does get in, it will give me an idea about the possession versus reanimation thing."

I have experience with possession. Ugly stuff. "Can I use the cross made of iron to tell if she's possessed, like I did with Reverend Stout?"

"You still have it?"

I would probably sleep with it if that wasn't super creepy. It's not exactly a fashion statement or a comforting object, in general. More like a last resort. "After what happened last month, you bet I do."

"I'm not sure if it would work, since nothing about this situation is normal. She has anchors like I've never seen."

"Can't hurt to try, can it?"

She shrugs, noncommittal. "Get it for me, and if I have the chance, I'll use it on her."

I feel better. At least we have a plan.

Logan enters, sees Sage now eating the remains of his breakfast, after pushing my plate aside, and frowns. "Guess I'm done."

Refilling his coffee and mine, I hand him the single biscuit she hasn't touched. "Everything okay?"

"No." He accepts them and grabs a napkin. "The judge had an unexpected family emergency out of town. He won't be back until Thursday."

I start to protest, then glance at Sage. "But he prepared the you-know-what, right?"

Logan shakes his head. "We can't you-know-what until Saturday morning now, I'm afraid."

Sage wipes her mouth. "I know you're getting hitched, and by the way, you stink at speaking in code." She pushes back the chair and gathers the cameras. "I'll get started on installing these."

Logan gives me a quizzical look as we allow her to pass. "Why do we need those?"

I do an impression of Trysta. "Logi, what do you think of my cupcakes?" I bat my eyelashes.

He chuckles. "Those will help?"

"Ye of little faith!" Sage calls from the front door.

"She's really got to you, hasn't she?" Logan asks.

Sighing, I begin cleaning up the plates. "With everything else going wrong at the moment, we need all the help we can get."

Seeing my dismay over the delayed license, he sets down his cup and squeezes my shoulder. "It's only an extra few days."

"About that," I say, rinsing the plates. "Maybe we should tell your mom."

His brows shoot up to his hairline. "And unleash Armageddon?"

"I'm feeling bad about keeping it from her."

He kisses my forehead. "Me, too. Let's talk about it tonight, okay?"

"Sure." I watch him head to his office, Arthur and Lancelot circling my legs, most likely in hopes there are scraps of leftovers.

"Sorry, boys," I tell them.

Seeing my dress might make me feel better, and regardless of whether I'm going to need it or not before the week is over, I can finish the seam work with Rhys and take that off Gloria's plate.

I snag the cross from my bedroom, gather my purse, and make sure Rosie is fine handling our morning appointment. She is and I give Sage the cross before I head to Gloria's to get my wedding gown.

FOUR

iss Jasmine's Bridal Boutique is owned by Gloria and managed by her business partner, Joseph. Gloria has kept her company small and exclusive, offering one-of-a-kind designs to a select clientele. While she produces a handful of gowns each season to be replicated and sold commercially by chain stores throughout the South, her main focus is exclusive and customized gowns for her elite brides.

I'm lucky Aunt Willa showed her my designs in the early stages and she offered to create the prototypes for me. She has added three more seamstresses to her group so she can handle my orders.

Brynlee, her bridal consultant, looks alarmed when I enter. A party of women are in the posh showroom, the potential bride and her mother arguing in French. "Miss Fantome, how lovely to see you," Brynlee says. "I'm afraid Gloria isn't here. May I help you?"

"I know Gloria is under the weather. I'm on my way to see her, but I wanted to swing by and pick up my gown."

"Your what?" Brynlee glances at the tablet in her hands,

scrolling hurriedly through her notes. "I don't have you down today."

"It's okay," I assure her. "I'm sure it's not on your appointments. Gloria was working on it for me personally. She probably has it in back."

Brynlee seems relieved, but only for a moment as the argument between the women grows more heated. We glance at the pair, and Brynlee lowers her voice. "Can you help? Please? I hate to ask, but they can't agree on which gown is *the one*." She makes air quotes. "I'm afraid they're going to leave with neither!"

The mother drips pearls, her daughter, diamonds. The gowns in question are displayed on side-by-side mannequins and I can see the custom-made quality. They are equally beautiful. "I'm afraid I don't speak French," I tell her, grateful I can sidestep the plea.

Her face brightens and she drags me over anyway. "They speak English."

I plaster on a smile as I'm introduced. The perfumed air, heavy with tension, nearly chokes me as two sets of matching deep brown eyes assess me from head to toe. The bride is named Marisol, her mother, Patrice.

"Miss Fantome is a designer, like Gloria. A close friend, too." Brynlee is in full showboat mode. "She's an expert on these things."

Marisol seems relieved. Patrice frowns. I've been caught plenty of times between brides and well-meaning family members. It's never a comfortable thing, yet it comes with the territory.

Taking a deep breath, I exam the displayed gowns and then the bride. The design labeled Tiffany has long layers of satin, with a slim profile and generous neckline. Yards of smooth satin flow from the train. Totally elegant, and ideal for the Marisol's tall, model-like frame. The other I have not seen before, but is labeled Belle of the Ball. The hourglass shape, with off the shoulder sleeves, a full skirt, and thousands of fine crystals covering the bodice, would be equally stunning on her. "Which do you feel special in?" I ask her.

Marisol's gaze darts to the Tiffany and back to her mother, but she doesn't meet Patrice's eyes. In heavily accented English, she remains noncommittal. "Each is exquisite."

Which loosely translates to *mom is paying* and *I want her to be happy*.

Being miserable at her own expense, however, isn't fair. I understand the quandary, living my own version of my happiness verses my mother-in-law's.

Motioning her forward, I lead her to stand in front of the mannequins. I place one of her hands on the Tiffany. "Close your eyes and imagine the day of the ceremony," I instruct. "Visualize yourself walking the aisle in this."

Her mouth, lips heavily coated in dark cherry red lipstick, turns up at the corners. She gently strokes the material.

I continue painting the picture. "Your groom is waiting and his eyes grow wide as he sees you in it. You're the woman he loves and wants to spend the rest of his life with."

Her smile grows and she lovingly caresses the material. "It is perfection."

Without glancing at her mother, I guide her hand to the Belle. "Now imagine wearing this gown. Same scenario. See yourself walking the aisle, all eyes on you. It's your day."

The smile falters. Her hand is stiff on the bodice, nails clicking against the crystals.

A quick glance at Patrice, and I see deep wrinkles have appeared around her mouth.

"One more visualization," I say, hoping to save the day for both of them, Brynlee, *and* Gloria. "Imagine the reception. You and your beloved stroll into the glamorous setting, the lights of the room reflecting off these crystals as though you, yourself, are lit from within. This gown offers plenty of room to move, dance, laugh. Elegant but fun."

Marisol's eyes pop open. "*C'est magnifique!*" She spins. "Ma mére, I need the pair. One for the ceremony and one for the reception. *D'accord?*"

Patrice gives me a challenging glare. Her lips purse as she thinks it over and I find myself holding my breath. Slowly and with reserve, she nods once. "*Trés bien.* We take both."

Marisol squeals, startling me, and throws her arms around my neck. Her bridesmaids join in a dance as Brynlee does her own squeal, and then straightens her sheath dress. She taps at the tablet as the young women form a ring around the gowns and sing something in French. "I'll get the details taken care of." She smiles at Patrice. "All I need is your credit card."

As the mother fishes in her handbag, Brynlee glides past the white marble counter and points at the door leading to the work room. "Joseph should be back there," she tells me. "I owe you."

"It was my pleasure." I'm relieved Gloria didn't lose the sale. "But I do accept donations of peach pie from The Beehive if you're ever in my neighborhood."

"I'll get you ten," she says.

The noise of sewing machines, overhead music, and Joseph's booming voice greets me as I enter the workspace. He waves when he sees me and gets up from his desk, talking to someone through his Bluetooth. The women at the machines don't glance up, all of them working furiously on gowns in various stages of completion.

I meet him at a worktable as he ends the conversation. Always dressed in black, today is no exception. His salt and pepper hair is slicked away from his face and he uses a black handkerchief to wipe moisture from his balding head. He tugs the device from his ear. "Avalon, to what do we owe the pleasure? Have you come to fill in for Gloria?"

"Already did." I hook a thumb over my shoulder toward the showroom and grin. "Actually, I'm here to pick up a gown of mine she was altering. I understand it's not finished, but with her sick, I figured I could complete the job myself. I'm sort of on a deadline for it."

His brows dip. "Oh, yes, *that* gown." He messes around with the fabric before him, and I wonder if Gloria divulged it was for my wedding. "How much sewing experience do you have? It might be better to wait for Gloria to return."

My stomach sinks. "Why is that?"

"It was more than a few simple alterations, I'm afraid."

"No, no." I shake my head. He must be thinking of another gown. "I needed the chest let out half an inch on each side and the length taken up. That's all."

He splays his hands wide. "She did more than that."

"What?" I cling to the hope he's confused. "How much more?"

Seemingly embarrassed, he leads me to another station far in the back. This is Gloria's personal work place, decorated with plants and swatches of beautiful material. There's a chalkboard and pictures of things that inspire her—butterflies, the Eiffel Tower, a photo of her parents.

On the lovely marble table is a gown in multiple pieces. I gasp as I recognize the details, the added bling. "Why?" is all I manage to say.

He points at the different sections. "She moved the zipper from the back to the side for ease of getting in and out of. She also had to adjust the arm holes when she added the extra fabric to the bust."

I'm flabbergasted and dismayed. There's no way I can

reconstruct the entire garment. Not even if I had from now until October. "Oh, Gloria."

"It will be even more stunning when she is finished." He gives me a hopeful smile. "Functional, too. She always talks about how you love that."

It's true. "She knows me well. I'll..." *Figure something out.* What choice do I have? Doesn't seem like there's going to be a wedding anyway.

His desk phone rings, his Bluetooth lighting up. "I'm sorry."

I force a smile. "No problem. I need to run. Thank you anyway."

A ghost of an older woman clings to Marisol. She makes eye contact and speaks in French. I hear *grandmére* and she stops me before I can make it out the door. "Tell her to wear the sapphire and diamond drop earrings," she says, switching to English. "They are in her father's safe. A family heirloom. They match her eyes."

Being who I am—*what* I am—I don't protest much anymore when these things happen. However, I do keep my mediumship abilities on the down low when I can. Marisol and her companions aren't from these parts, though, and I know I'll regret it if I don't relay the message.

Brynlee calls "goodbye" and I wave at her before pulling the bride aside to repeat the information about the jewels. Her startled expression turns joyful, yet slightly disbelieving. "How could you know about them?"

"I'm a medium," I explain. "Good luck with the wedding."

Escaping to my car before she or her entourage can ask more questions, I grip the steering wheel so hard I give myself a hand cramp. The important thing is that Gloria is all right, not that I can't wear my gown at my wedding.

IF I have a wedding.

I put the car in gear and head for Betty's to pick up flowers.

Our local florist is busy, her new shop on the edge of town doing a brisk business. I select a lovely summer arrangement from the cooler and ask her to add a few silky butterflies to it. She has ones that match the irises in the bouquet. Soon, I'm on my way to the hospital.

FIVE

Like many people, I avoid hospitals as much as possible. For me, being able to see and hear ghosts makes them even more uncomfortable. The smells and sounds of the place assault me, including the screech of the ambulance siren bringing someone to the ER. Some of the ghosts ignore me, caught in time loops where they reenact what happened to them; others too caught up in their own world to realize I can see them.

The volunteer at the front desk gives me Gloria's room number. Avoiding eye contact with various spirits, I make my way to the bank of elevators. It's better to pretend I can't see and hear them. Before I leave, I will make the mental lighted doorway my friend and fellow ghost whisperer, Winter, has taught me to do. Any of those souls wishing to cross over will be able to.

An elderly man climbs in with me and eyes the flowers. He's probably in his sixties, his shirt wrinkled, and he smells of Old Spice aftershave. "My wife loves irises." He points to those in the arrangement. "Our backyard is full of them."

He speaks of her in the present tense, but the spirit hovering around him, attempting to tidy his unkempt hair and press the wrinkles out of his shirt, suggests she's passed on. Her hands go right through him, but she keeps trying, and at one point, he reaches up and touches his head, as if he feels her. "Tell him he needs a haircut," she says in a loving but scolding tone.

I fiddle with a butterfly. "I hope my friend likes them, too."

He glances around, looking for a fly or whatever he imagines is tickling him. "I bring a few to Laney every day. Keep hoping she'll wake up, and I want them to be the first thing she sees. Outside of my handsome face, that is." He winks.

Wakes up? I assess the ghost. "What happened?"

She starts to respond, but so does he, drowning her out. "Fell down the stairs, hit her head." His face is contrite. "I told her I'd take care of the laundry, but she's always been so independent. She never listens to me or lets anyone help her. She twisted an ankle, sent the basket flying, and toppled down a whole flight. Dang, woman."

Laney smacks his arm. He looks down at the spot. She's got enough juice, it seems, to create some solidity in her hands. Interesting. I hope she does wake, but I sense she may already be too far on the other side.

We arrive at the second floor and he gives me a sad smile. "You take care, young lady."

"You, too," I say to both of them.

In Gloria's room, a monitor beeps softly and rhythmically. Her eyes are closed and her breathing is even, but her face is pale and drawn. She's always been vivacious; it's a shock to see her this way.

I place the flowers next to another bouquet on the substantial windowsill. The blinds are closed and the wall AC lazily blows the leaves around, causing the butterflies on their wires to appear as though they are real, buzzing about the petals.

She doesn't stir, lost in sleep. An IV pumps fluid into her system and I say a prayer for her health. A nurse enters a minute later to take her vitals. "You family?"

Her scrub top is covered with cartoon cats and her head has recently been shaved. "A friend. How is she?"

"Better once we pumped her stomach. Lost a lot of fluid and all that vomiting upended her electrolytes."

"I know food poisoning can be serious, but I still expected her to be sitting up giving you all grief and demanding to be discharged. She's always so...alive. I've never seen her like this."

She records something on a folded piece of paper drawn from her pocket. "The electrolyte imbalance affected her heart. Once she's rehydrated and we've got that under control, she'll feel a lot better. Probably be released by this evening."

"Really?" I stare at Gloria's wan face. "Could you call me if she is? I'd like to be the one to pick her up."

She wraps a blood pressure cuff around Gloria's slender arm. "Leave your number at the desk. I'm done at three, but I'll make a note for my replacement to contact you."

The machine kicks in and the cuff inflates. Even this does not rouse the patient. "Thank you. Have they figured out what she ate that caused this?"

She watches the monitor until it's finished and makes another note while the device deflates. "We've ruled out the likely culprits—fish and other meats—since she claims she never had any. The results of the tests aren't back yet, but bacteria and other sources are in everything these days. Salad fixings, eggs, nuts, you name it." Her hands are gentle as she removes the cuff. Her shoes squeak as she heads for the door. "'Just as long as it wasn't my dessert' she said to me." A chuckle. "Claimed she refuses to give up her sweets."

My stomach drops. "Did she say what the dessert was?"

The nurse opens the door, shaking her head. Voices from the hall trickle in. "Chocolate was all she mentioned, saying it was her addiction."

The door shuts on silent hinges, and I make a note as well, mine mental. I text Rosie first, but she doesn't know what Gloria might have eaten for dessert last night. I call Joseph and get the same answer.

I kiss Gloria's cheek and leave my number at the nurses' station. Jumping to conclusions is pointless; Trysta isn't even officially open for business yet. But when my friend rouses, I plan to make sure she's not one of the deadly ghost's targets.

At my parents' home, the lawn is half mowed and a flower bed of Mama's is in the process of getting new mulch. She's at City Hall, working, but Daddy's here, his truck in the drive.

I don't see him anywhere, and when I'm on the front porch, I hear the strains of music. His, to be precise, filtering out of an upstairs window.

It was once Mama's craft room, filled with fabrics, paints, and yarn. She's always taking up a new hobby, at least in theory, but never has time to start a project, much less finish any. My parents were separated for years, and since Daddy's return, he's commandeered it, installing acoustic tiles, a speaker system, and lighting for video recording sessions.

My father was once a police officer in town, but his heart has always been about music. When he left, he became a rock musician, and still has quite the following.

The song is a haunting melody, and as I let myself in the door and ascend the stairs, I wonder if he's practicing or recording. Either way, his voice is comforting, pitch perfect, even when he purposely lowers it and gives it a dramatic rasp. By the time I hit the landing, the final chords drift on the air and I hear him pause for a heartbeat before he begins speaking. "What do you think? Let me know in the comments."

I peek my head in and he glances up from his laptop. A grin breaks over his face. There's a high-tech camera with built-in microphone attached to the computer, and he continues his monologue, as he waves me in. "That was totally off-the-cuff, and I'll be fine-tuning it for Saturday night at the Palladium in Atlanta. Don't wait to grab your tickets—they're going fast, and seating is limited. I'll be playing that new tune, along with a mix of my greatest hits. All proceeds go to the Peachtree Girls and Boys Club, so please come out and support a great group helping our youth. I'm counting on you." He raises his pick. "I have a few dozen of these to give away to some lucky fans. Ones I've used in concert. Every donation over fifty dollars gets one, until they run out. If you can't make it in person, you can still donate, and I'll drop the link in the comments. Be safe, be kind, and rock on, my friends! See you Saturday." He clicks off with a smile and hands me his guitar.

"New song?" I ask.

His hair is mussed from running his hands through it. His T-shirt and jeans stained from the dirt. "The muse struck when I was hands deep in the flowerbed. I needed to record it before my old brain let it get away."

I kiss his cheek. "You're not old."

"You're too kind." He scans the screen and types. "Just did a Facebook live session. First time I've tried it, but I think it went pretty well. Lots of hearts and positive comments so far."

"That's great, Daddy."

Removing the attached camera unit, he gets up and places it in an open case. "I'm glad you're here. Let me upload the tract to YouTube and I'll be right down, okay?"

It's cool to have a dad who's a star, although I didn't always embrace it. I mosey downstairs, glancing over the family pictures lining the wall, and smiling over the undone projects outside. That's my dad one-hundred-percent.

Growing up, he would write lyrics and riffs only he could hear on anything available—scraps of paper, dirty napkins, receipts he fished from a pocket. Once, he used Mama's favorite lipstick to write a chorus on the bathroom mirror. If he didn't get them down immediately, he'd forget them. He was a cop then, and Mama, being the Type A personality she is, hated it. Any projects she asked him to do around the place were often left incomplete and unfinished because, like today, he'd tackle cleaning the gutters or painting a wall and suddenly be overcome with inspiration.

He joins me in the kitchen a few minutes later where I've poured him a glass of sweet tea. His fans don't care about his disheveled look. In fact, this is what they love—seeing Daddy being his natural, raw self. No pretense, no fancy clothes, just a laid-back style and honest talent. "I finally made headway on Trysta."

"The first good news I've had today." Since he still has contacts in the force and a nose for investigation, I'd asked him to do a background check on her to start. That had turned up only one suspicious fact—her name and identity hadn't appeared in any database until three years ago. But she had a clean record, not even a parking ticket to her name.

I follow him to Mama's study and hastily slide a coaster under the sweating glass when he goes to plunk it down. He rifles through a stack of manila folders, his scrawled handwriting on the label tabs. "It's here somewhere."

Finding the one he wants, he yanks it out and hands it to me. I clutch it tightly. "Please tell me she's a wanted criminal and we can have her in jail by nightfall. She's upping her game and it worries me immensely."

Laughter crinkles the corners of his eyes. "Afraid I haven't discovered anything worthy of jail time. Yet," he adds. "I did pick up a thin trail. She's good at hiding her tracks, but I'm better at uncovering them." He winks.

"You bet your guitar pick you are." I flip open the folder and see copies of business paperwork filed with the state. I rifle through the pages of legalese. "What does this tell me?"

The Thornhollow police force lost a great cop when my father left and formed a band. His heart was always with his music, but I believe it accelerated his analytical skills and imagination. He could outthink and outwit any criminal around. "Since I couldn't find record of her existence beyond three years ago, I looked up her business tax filings and followed the money. Discovered she's financed this bakery with funds from her previous life." He stands beside me and shuffles through the papers, pulling one out and placing it on top. "She's formerly Stacey Bollinger Lambert, stepdaughter of West Virginia sugar tycoon Larry Lambert. Twelve years ago, he got cancer but went into remission days before he was struck by lightning and fell into a coma."

"Cancer *and* a lightning strike?" What are the odds of that? "Yikes. Sounds like bad karma."

"It gets worse. His wife died a few weeks later in a car accident that the police suspected was suicide. Stacey was in the car, but lived. Her only relative was her grandmother, Mabel, who was on *her* deathbed. She passed a month later, Stacey was an orphan again and the court placed her in foster care. She bounced around between homes, then went off the grid. She was fifteen at the time. Police believe she ran away."

"No death record?"

"That's an interesting part of this. A woman's body matching her description turned up in Mexico a few years later, but get this. The coroner claims she got up and walked out of the morgue."

"*No.*"

He rubs his hands together, as if enjoying the juicy story. "Crazy, right?"

So is she a ghost or isn't she? "They're sure it was her?"

H shrugs. "No one really cared if it was or not. They had more pressing matters to take care of, and the case was closed."

"And she returned to the States and became Trysta Harding."

He pulls out another sheet, this one with a grainy photocopy of a birth certificate. "The thing is, the social security number I dug up for Stacey belongs to Mabel. I couldn't find a birth certificate for Mabel, but she had two wealthy husbands during her lifetime. One was a doctor who treated her after she was…get this…struck by lightning at eleven years old. He was fascinated with her case and eventually married her when she came of age."

"Eww."

"He and her second husband both ended up in comas."

"This just gets weirder and weirder."

"You're going to love this." He digs through his notes and finds what he's looking for. "According to the police report, the doctor was performing an experiment to replicate the original lightning strike to Mabel and ended up getting toasted himself, while she was left without a scratch."

"He experimented on her?"

"Put him in a coma."

"And her second husband? How did he end up in one?"

He sips more tea and runs a finger over the page. "This doesn't fit the profile exactly, but he was accidentally electrocuted while trying to fix a light in their kitchen."

"Was it during a storm?"

Daddy shrugs. "No mention in the report."

"It put him in a coma?"

"Apparently. Both men are alive but neither has woken up in all these years."

A chill runs through me. "Is Larry Lambert alive?"

"Yes, but he's never regained consciousness, either. His sugar empire had to be sold off several years ago to pay the medical bills." Daddy finishes his drink. "This is better than that true crime podcast I love. I'll keep digging, see if I can find more."

I came here to pick his brain about my wedding situation, but my problems have to wait. I need to think through this connection with lightning and electricity and focus on stopping Trysta/Stacey before she takes her next victim. "If I show the social security number to Detective Jones, can he arrest Trysta for identity theft? She's obviously not Mabel."

"It's weak. Duplicates are rare, but data entry errors do happen, and a half-decent lawyer could get her off those charges."

"But it's her grandmother's."

"Would that solve your ghost problem?"

"Might slow her down with Chuck, at least."

He pats my arm. "Let me see if I can find something more substantial. When you're going after someone like this, the first strike is critical. After that, they know you're gunning for them. Makes it a whole lot messier."

I hand the folder back to him and kiss his cheek. "You're amazing and I can't thank you enough." At least it's more than I had, even if I'm still unsure how to save Charles and force this ghost—and all her attached spirits—to cross.

He calls to me as I head for the door. "See you at the book club!"

I stop with my hand on the knob. "Mama roped you in?"

He follows me out to the yard. "I can never say no to her, you know that."

"None of us can." I point at the bed. "It will look great when it's finished."

"If I ever get rid of all the dollar weed." He kicks at a pile of limp greenery, their tubers white against the orange clay and black topsoil. "I swear some of them have root systems that run clear to Florida and back."

"Overachievers," I snarl at them. Just like my mother. "Did you actually read the book?"

"We read it together." He glances around like she might be watching. "A chapter a night for the past month. Then we had to discuss it. In great depth. Believe me, I'm thoroughly versed on everything from the character arcs to the author's skill at using metaphors. Give me a good John Grisham title over that any day."

I laugh and hug him bye before I head for home.

SIX

A modicum of hope restored after my visit; I feel even better when I arrive at The Wedding Chapel to find Sage finishing the installation of the cameras.

A red truck is parked out front, *Quigg Construction* painted on the sides and tailgate. The father and son team of Evan and Bis come and go these days, restoring the old homestead down the hill near the creek where Sam and Tabby lived when they founded Thornhollow all those years ago.

The gargoyle cats on the posts chatter constantly as Sage gathers up her cordless screwdriver and sticks it in her bag. "She's good," one says to me as I ascend the steps.

"You know it," she replies.

I stop on the landing, not surprised she, too, can hear my inanimate objects. The cameras are tucked over the outside lights but visible. "Did Trysta see you?"

"Ha," the door knocker says with smug glee. "She sure did!"

Sage grins and glances at the bakery. "I went over and asked her to help, in fact. Told her what I was doing and said I needed to check the angles of them so I could pick up the sidewalk. As suspected, she told me she was too busy. She just doesn't want to be caught on video. Imagine that." She smirks. "And now she knows she will if she ventures over here."

More good news. Maybe today won't go down in flames after all. "You're sneaky and I love it. Could you tell if she's possessing the body or really is a ghost?"

"Afraid not. I tried handing her the cross and she wouldn't take it. She did have her hands coated in flour at the time. Could be an indication of possession, but not a strong one."

I'd like to take the cross and put it you know where. "Come inside and let me pay you."

At my desk, she brings up the security software and walks me through the settings and options. "The cameras are motion-sensitive, but you can change it to have them record continuously if you want. That will drain the batteries faster, but it's up to you. In case she, or anyone else, tries to tamper with them, I've put a protection spell on them, and also hid two more in the second floor flower boxes. Unless she can fly, she won't be able to touch those." A few clicks and I'm looking at myself coming up the sidewalk. "If you switch to this option,"—she clicks a dropdown menu and the screen shades to a sickly green —"it will show any spectral activity."

Sure enough it does. Following me is a ghost.

My heart jumps when I realize who it is. "Aunt Willa!"

She gives a wave to the camera as if she knows she'll appear on the video, then floats around the side of the house, while I climb the front steps.

Sage stops the replay. "Didn't you see her walking with you?"

"I've only been able to see her a rare few times. Mostly, she talks to me, and even that's sporadic. It's so good to see her. Can you play it again?"

A cool, minty breeze tickles my nose and sweeps over my

shoulders. *"I'm always...with you."* My aunt's voice is static-filled, like a radio dial that can't bring in a station clearly. *"I watch after...you...and your mother."*

A loud beeping goes off. It's coming from the teddy bear, now on one of my bookshelves.

"The EMF meter," Sage says, going to the stuffed animal. She opens up its back and fiddles with it until the noise stops. "Who's here?"

"It's my aunt." Happiness floods my heart. I glance around, determined to see her spirit, but there's nothing, and I deflate a bit. "I miss you, Aunt Willa."

Rosie waddles in and we hear the back screen door slam. Moxley, who's been lying in a patch of sunlight on the wooden floor, raises his head to give a "woof," but lays back down when he sees it's Bis.

"I miss you, too, Miss Willa," Rosie says to the walls in my office. She can't hear or see spirits. "But your niece is doing an amazing job and I'm glad she's here."

"Thanks," I say, squeezing her lightly on the shoulder.

"Hey, Ava." Bis glances toward the bookshelf near Sage. "Hey, Miss Willa. Looking good! The other side treating you well?"

"Wait." I squint at the place he's staring at. "You can see her?"

He looks confused. "Can't you?"

I shake my head.

His gaze begins to track my aunt as she leaves the office and he leans around the corner. "Looks like she's headed outside. Probably to check on our progress." He faces me again. "She does that a lot."

Really? "I had no idea. That's nice."

"What are you working on today?" Rosie asks. Fern has

followed her and sniffs at one of Biz's pant cuffs. Moxley raises his head again and she goes to sniff his paws.

"The living room fireplace," he answers. "The chimney has several layers of bricks that are unstable due to lost mortar. We have to fill in those holes without toppling the upper section. It's very focused and time-consuming, but worth it to save the original structure. I don't like heights, so Dad does most of the work."

I'm still wondering about my aunt. "How is it you can see her and I can't?"

Bis doesn't miss a beat. "It's all frequency. Humans, in general, have a limited range for light, color, and sound. Most animals have broader ones and can see in the dark, or smell scents that we can't. A few of us have more bandwidth, so to speak, and can see, hear, and sense frequencies outside of the norm. My range is similar to yours, but distinct, as yours is to mine. Like our fingerprints or DNA, I believe we have individualized frequency waves that we give off and can also distinguish."

Sage clicks away at the keyboard. "Are you science-ing us?" Her tone is dry, as always, but I see a teasing spark in her eyes.

Bis grins in a way that tells me he's a goner for this girl. "You love it, and you know it. All your witchy, magical stuff isn't at odds with logic and deduction. It's basic science and physics, and I believe we'll see psychic phenomena and 'woo-woo' practices decoded and demystified in the next decade."

Sage makes a face, but she, too, is head over broomstick for this kid. I pay her for the security system and shoo them off. Rosie asks after Gloria and I fill her in, including my hope about her coming home today.

The afternoon flies by. Between clients and phone calls, I save the clip of Aunt Willa and replay it several times. I keep my eyes and ears peeled, thinking about Bis' assessment of why

I can't see her and wondering if there's a way to expand my range of frequencies. Every time I watch her spectral form wave at the camera, I smile. It brings me a sense of peace, regardless of the chaos around me.

Our last appointment of the day runs long and Rosie is fading fast, so I send her home and wrap up the meeting myself. After I close and lock the front door, I check on Logan.

His hair is standing on end as though he's run his fingers through it a dozen times. He sits back in the chair when I enter and tosses his favorite pen on the desktop. "I'm afraid I don't have time to help with dinner."

"One of those days, huh?"

He nods. "You, too?"

I check my watch. "It wasn't bad, but I'm running late. Book club is in an hour. Do you think I can get out of it?"

His expression gives me the answer. "Was it that bad?"

"I didn't read it," I admit. "I haven't had time."

He sits forward and does a search on his computer. "I'll print off a cheat sheet for you."

"A cheat sheet?"

"Yeah, from that one site... Here it is, Plot Twist. They list all the bestsellers that they've dissected."

I lean across the desk and kiss his forehead. "Just for that, I'll whip up something for us and we'll eat in here."

He grabs my arm and brings me in for a longer, much deeper lip-lock. When he releases me, we're both out of breath. "We make a good team, you know that?"

I smile. "The best."

"We'll figure out the right avenue to take with the wedding."

I hug him and he goes back to his work. In the kitchen, I make sandwiches and warm up leftover collard greens. He has the info ready and waiting when I return, and we briefly discuss our days as we eat. As we're finishing, I remember the other thing on my evening to-do list. "I haven't heard from the hospital."

"Call them." He wipes his hands on a napkin and balls it up, dropping it onto his empty plate. "Your message may have gotten lost in the shift change."

We gather the dishes and he helps me take them to the sink. The cats and Moxley are anxious for their dinners. While I call, he feeds them and listens in.

The receptionist looks up Gloria's name and confirms she's still a patient. I ask to be put through to her room, but the phone rings and rings. There's no option to get back to the switchboard, so I have to start over, but this time I request she transfer me to the nurses' station.

Logan loads the dishwasher as someone finally comes on over the speaker. The nurse informs me Gloria has had a setback. She's stable, but is dizzy and disoriented, so Dr. Ernestine is keeping her overnight. I thank her and hang up. "Poor Gloria."

He rubs my arm, seeing my concern. "She's a fighter. She'll be back to normal before you know it."

I hope that's true. Mama texts to tell me she's on the way to pick me up. I respond, letting her know that's not necessary. I can drive myself.

To no one's surprise, she insists. She'll be here in ten minutes. I ask about Daddy and she informs me he's recording a new song.

I'll just bet, but good for him for finding a way to bow out of tonight's get together. She doesn't seem upset, so I let it go.

Upstairs, I freshen up and grab the book from my nightstand. It actually looks like one I'd enjoy and I promise myself I'll read it. I grab a bag of supplies to cleanse Hannah's home, hoping I can bum a ride to and from there afterwards.

While I wait for Mama on the porch, continuing to scan for Aunt Willa, I scrutinize the detailed synopsis Logan printed for me. Each character's motivation is explained in-depth and the story's chain of events are laid out and evaluated. I just might make it through the meeting without divulging I haven't delved into it yet.

Persephone joins me. She's dressed in a bright orange skirt and Caribbean blue tank top. "I love that story. So gripping, and yet, it really makes you think about life as a whole, you know?"

"You read it?"

"Of course. We have book club meetings in Heaven, you know."

"Please assure me you aren't coming with me. You have angel stuff to do, right?"

She sits and rocks in a chair, even though she's incorporeal and shouldn't be able to make it move. "You might encounter a ghost at the library."

Speaking of. "Have you spotted the one haunting Hannah? I didn't see him hanging around her this morning, and Sam hasn't reported in. Maybe Sly is like Aunt Willa and my radar can't pick him up?"

A shake of her head and her eyes track my mother's car pulling to the curb. "There's more to that situation. Another reason I should attend tonight."

Oh goodie. I head down the steps, my mother waving at me to hurry. "Just don't distract me," I murmur through gritted teeth. "This is important for Mama. I need to not embarrass her. "

"Honey, I hate to break it to you,"—her skirt flutters around her ankles as she floats along the sidewalk ahead of me—"but that horse left the barn ages ago."

Across the street, I see the curtain flutter in the bakery

window. A shadow moves across the lighted opening. Before I get in, I text Logan. *Be sure you have the necklace on you at all times while I'm gone, k?*

I get in and Mama greets me. She's in her classic linen suit, a light shade of yellow this time. "I'm so excited! Our inaugural book club meeting. I've wanted to start one of these for so long."

Logan responds with a thumbs-up and a heart. Thank goodness he believes in me and what I do. "Seems like everybody is excited about it."

She backs out, chattering away, and I eye the bakery. I can't see Trysta, but I feel her watching us. Charles is strolling up the sidewalk and he waves. I return it, wishing I could simply tell him she's evil and he'd believe me.

"Don't worry," Persephone states, and I glance back to see her studying Charles. Trysta bursts out the front door and throws her arms around him, her gaze following us as we drive away. "Logan is safe. Tonight," she adds.

SEVEN

The two-story brick library welcomes us with the warm glow of Victorian streetlights illuminating the sidewalk and wood and glass double doors, which are propped open.

By the half-full parking lot, I expect a good crowd. I'm not disappointed when we enter and a cheer goes up for my mother. She waves it off, loving every second of it, and I'm left on my own as she takes center stage. At the head of the long, walnut table Baylor has prepared, she opens her book to remove a sheet of questions. Attendees jockey to get a seat near her; the rest fill a selection of chairs placed nearby.

Baylor greets me, and a few others gesture or nod to acknowledge my presence. I'm working my way to a chair in the far corner, playing the dutiful daughter and thankful I'm not in the spotlight, when I feel someone's focus on me.

Helen Cross is seated at the other end of the table and the corners of her eyes crease as she studies my jeans and t-shirt.

Stupid of me to think she'd miss out on this. When it comes to knowing everything that happens in our sleepy Southern community, she and Mama are in close competition. Helen tweaks the edge of her mouth in what might pass for a long-suffering smile and I return a more dogged one. Rosie is right—I need to do everything I can to keep whatever regard I've earned with her.

Once seated, I notice movement out of the corner of my eye and see Hannah leaning forward to peek past another attendee. "Good to see you," she whispers.

Sam floats behind her, taking in the historical section. I touch my bag, now hanging on the chair. "Are we still on for after the meeting?"

She nods, and Mama clears her throat. "Ava?" Mama pins me with an expectant look. "Why don't you start us off?" She places reading glasses on the tip of her nose and selects the first question on her list. "In the opening scene, did you believe the main character was speaking about herself or her twin sister?"

I swallow and try to recall if the synopsis mentioned this. Nothing pops into my head. "I found it evocative and the voice of the author pulled me right into the story." I continue, working around the question and using words from the reviewers who added comments after the recap. One of them mentioned the duplicity of the opening chapter and I assume she was referring to this. "At first I believed it was regarding Pansy, but as I read further, I considered it could be referring to either her or Pauline."

Mama smiles, delighted. I've never been able to pull a fast one on her, and guilt will make me confess later, sure as the Methodist church bells ring every Sunday, but for now, Dixie Fantome is happy. When Mama's happy, I'm happy. She winks at me before she surveys those gathered. "Anyone else realize we were inside Pauline's head in the opening scene?"

Several hands shoot up and I relax. The night goes on, the attendees discussing the characters and suspenseful elements in great detail. Persephone pops in and out, adding her comments that only I and Sam can hear, but she's generally well-behaved. Most folks loved the story; only two criticize it. Since Mama seems to have enjoyed it immensely, this is at their own peril.

During a break, before we vote on next month's selection, Hannah leaves to use the restroom. I follow, just to stretch my legs, and linger near the mystery section, pretending to examine an exhibit of summer-themed reads while I once again search for Sylvester. Baylor has used a round table and covered it with a cloth printed with cheery sunflowers. The novels include steamy romances, women's lit, and humorous beach reads.

Sam joins me. "This library is miraculous. We had such limited books and papers in my day."

"Any sight of Sly?" I whisper.

He shakes his head. "Upon surveillance, I did observe a blue automobile following Hannah off and on today."

It's a small town. Could be coincidence, and ghosts don't need cars to get around. "Did you get a look at the driver?"

He runs a finger across several spines, reading the titles. "It was a young woman with similar features."

A relative? I file that away to ask her about later.

Helen approaches and I mentally groan, but greet her with a smile. "Ava," she says, "you seem distracted. Who are you talking to?"

She knows I commune with the dead. "Myself," I lie, and eye the summer reading display. "You didn't say much during the discussion. Did you not like the story?"

"The ending was melodramatic." She lifts her regal nose. "I've read superior quality literature."

"You don't want to miss voting for next month's selection then." I hope she'll take the hint and return to the meeting. "One of those quality literary books sounds great."

She sees through my attempt to get rid of her. "What do you like to read? We've never discussed your preferences."

This is a serious matter for the well-bred and well-read matriarch of the Cross empire. Out of the corner of my eye, I see a shadow and turn my head. It disappears behind a wooden unit of shelves filled with large print books. "I read across many genres." This is the truth. "However, with everything currently going on, I'm lucky to see more than my horoscope before I fall asleep at night."

My humor is lost on her. "Logan seems extremely busy, or perhaps preoccupied, since moving in with you."

She knows how much work he has, but I reiterate it anyway, brushing off the dig about me being the cause. "Since he's the only attorney in town, and the best one in these parts, he's up to his eyeballs most days. He's handling everything from wills and estate planning to business filings and divorce court appearances."

She rolls over that, facing the table. "Yet previously, he's always had time to take my calls."

I shift to the other side and feign interest in a beach read. "Did you leave a message?"

Her mouth firms and she picks up the classic *A Midsummer Night's Dream* by Shakespeare. "I did. He hasn't returned it."

Probably for good reason, since he's keeping our secret, and in general, doesn't have free time for chitchat about what brand of designer curtains she's purchasing or the latest variety of grapes the vineyard is planting. These are subjects she's been known to discuss ad infinitum with him. "I'm sure he was simply distracted before he could carve out a few minutes to devote to you. Would you like me to remind him when I get home?"

A sniff and her fingers worry the diamond bracelet on her

wrist. She moves to examine the same shelf of books Sam is gawking over. "I wish to discuss this with both of you, actually. I'll prepare dinner tomorrow night and you will be my guests."

Super. *I can hardly wait.* I force another smile as I scramble for an excuse, but I find none that seem legitimate, and like my mother, Helen has some type of internal radar that goes off when anyone lies. "How generous of you."

She gives me a skeptical glance, but appears satisfied. "Aren't you going to ask what it's about?"

My grandfather chuckles. "You are a patient and charitable woman, Avalon. She is a troublesome one." He eyes the books with longing. "I do wish I were human again so I could read these."

I remember Persephone's quip about book clubs in heaven. If Sam would cross over, he might be able to attend.

The restroom door opens and the old wooden floor squeaks as Hannah crosses the expanse. I gird myself and decide I might as well give in and play Helen's game. I wonder if she's somehow discovered our plans and intends to confront me here and now. "I'm always interested in anything you wish to talk about."

Another skeptical look, but she smiles at the edition in front of her. "We must plan an engagement party for Charles and Trysta. It will be tough to keep it a secret, but I'd like it to be a surprise."

I could not be less excited, but I'm relieved it's about them. By all accounts, it seems our secret is safe. "Yes, of course."

"Hello?" I hear Hannah call behind us. "Is someone there?"

I can't see her, and as Helen continues to go on about whether we should hold the party at the Country Club or the vineyard, I walk to peer across the short distance to the restrooms.

Hannah is nowhere to be seen. I hear her feet on the floorboards once more. "The light switch is on the left," she calls, and I realize she's at the top of stairs around the corner that lead to the computer area and children's section on the lower floor.

"Hannah?" I call.

The next thing I know, she screams and the sound of her tumbling down the steps causes Helen and I to exchange a horrified glance. Together, we run to the landing.

Sam floats down the steps. "Oh, dear," he says.

Since it's past visiting hours, the ground floor is closed and steeped in darkness. I hurry down the creaky wooden steps in the dark, Sam's vague glow showing me the way. "Hannah? Are you okay?"

The poor woman groans. I find her crumpled at the bottom.

Persephone appears. "What just happened?"

"You tell me," I mutter.

Helen, who followed at a more careful pace, fumbles for the wall switch, and when the overhead light floods the area, I blink at the glare reflected off the tiled floor. Hannah's already injured arm is pinned under her, her right leg twisted at an unnatural angle. There's blood running from her nose. "Call 911," I order.

Helen hustles back up the steps to get her phone. Hannah is conscious but dazed. She tries to turn onto her back and whimpers in pain.

"Don't move," I say. "Help is on the way."

She ignores my suggestion and manages to roll over, shutting her eyes against the light. "He...pushed...me."

"Who?" I glance around. "Sly?"

Her head moves in what appears to be confirmation but she winces and a tear slips from the corner of an eye. Her nose is bleeding profusely, running into her hair.

Sam rises approximately a foot off the ground, inspecting

every corner. "I'm afraid I've seen no evidence to support that claim."

"Me either," Persephone agrees.

"I'm going to grab some wet paper towels." I gently pat Hannah's arm. "I'll be right back."

By the time I return, others have come to see what's going on. In the distance, a siren wails. Sam has disappeared. Mama is beside herself and frets over Hannah. "How did this happen?"

"I'm not sure." I hold the towels to the injured woman's nose. Her cheek is beginning to swell, more tears flowing. I scan the computer bank and the section of the children's library visible from here. "I need to check something."

Mama takes the wet towels from my hands and doctors Hannah's face, leaning toward me and lowering her voice. "She told me someone pushed her."

I meet my mother's worried expression. "I didn't see anyone." Ghost or otherwise. "I'll look around."

She gets my drift and snaps off a nod. "Go."

First, I race through the children's area, confirming no one is present. I wonder what Hannah heard that would make her believe someone was here?

Helen is keeping the crowd back. I thread my way through those gathered on the steps and landing, everyone asking for details. The ambulance arrives, and so does a local cop. I avoid him and the paramedics, catching the faintest scent of old coffee lingering around the restroom. Several folks are hovering there and I figure it belongs to one of them.

Upstairs, I find Sam and Persephone in the main room. The table and chairs are still covered with copies of tonight's book selection, along with other personal items.

The two of them have their heads together. I approach and whisper, "Is Sylvester here?"

Persephone looks up. "There are a few ghosts in the place, but he's not among them."

"There are?" I haven't seen any. At her nod, I shake it off. That's for another time. "If not Sly, then who pushed Hannah down the steps?"

"I'm afraid we don't know," Sam answers. "Whoever it was slipped in and out under our combined noses."

The library has no security cameras. They've never been necessary. Regardless, I comb the rows of books, searching for any sign, spectral or human, that might suggest the identity of our culprit. I catch sight of a few of the ghosts Persephone mentioned, but they give me a wide berth.

Helen finds me in the romance section. "What in heaven's name are you doing?"

"Trying to find who did this."

"Don't be dramatic. She twisted her ankle and fell. Meantime, Detective Jones wishes to take our statements."

"Why is he here?"

"Apparently, he was in the neighborhood and heard the sirens."

This night just went from bad to worse. Girding myself once more, I motion to her. "Lead the way."

EIGHT

"Miss Hannah claims she was pushed." Jones is a beefy guy, a former high school linebacker. Instead of his normal uniform, tonight he wears a t-shirt that stretches across his muscular chest and emphasizes his biceps, along with faded jeans. We could be twins, outside of our different skin tones and his burly attitude. "Did you see anyone?"

The uniform hides a lot. I've never realized just how sizable he is. "No."

His stare tells me he doesn't like my short answer. I learned a long time ago not to offer more than a yes or no unless absolutely necessary. That's what happens when you have a cop for a dad. "You and Mrs. Cross were the only folks near her."

Coming from him, it's an accusation. "Yes."

Another stare that would make most people cower. By the look on his face, it's a good thing Helen and I can alibi each other. "Yet, you say you saw nothing."

Helen steps to my side. "We've both stated that several times, Landon."

He flicks his gaze to her and back to me. He makes a note

on the small pad he carries. With great patience and detachment, he questions me again. "Is there anything else you can tell me that might help sort this out? This is the second time in the past two weeks Mrs. Grady has sustained a serious injury from an accident." The last word is emphasized with a tone of doubt. "Is it possible she needs medical intervention for an illness?"

"Illness?" I'm puzzled. "What are you saying?"

"Are you aware of any inner ear infections, recent ailments, vertigo? Mental health issues?"

Mama budges in. "Don't be ridiculous, Landon. She's as sane and healthy as you are."

Even big, bad Detective Jones fears my mother to a certain extent. He holds up the hand with his pen as if in surrender. "It's my responsibility to cover all the angles, Miss Dixie. You know that."

"She tripped and fell," Helen states firmly. "The landing and stairs were dark. That's all."

"But she did call out to someone," I tell him. "She thought she heard a person down there."

He pauses, then writes. "And was there?"

"No. I checked."

He quizzes us for another minute, but we have nothing else to offer. Closing his notepad, he saunters off to interrogate the others, including Baylor, who is wringing her hands.

Mama trails after him. Helen pulls me aside. "Did you see a...you know?"

She can't even bring herself to say the word 'ghost.' "No. I thought it might be that, too, but I can't confirm one did this. There are a few spirits here and I did notice a shadow near us before it happened, but...?" I shrug.

"Do they cast shadows?" she asks. "Could it be some evil entity?"

Sly may be dangerous, and I've encountered my share of nasty spirits, but I haven't sensed anything that would qualify as evil here. "Maybe, like you said, she simply fell."

Helen seems overly relieved. "That must be it."

Since Hannah can't take me to her house, and Mama will be staying to help Baylor clean up, I go out on a limb. "I'd like to check out Hannah's house. Care to join me?"

The offer shocks her as much as it does me. "Do you have a key?"

"No, but I need to check the place, regardless."

"You're breaking in?" She shakes her head adamantly, then seems to think it over. "I can't get arrested."

She's not against committing a crime, just getting caught. *Interesting.* "I respect that. You can stay in the car, but I really need a ride."

"I'd be an accessory."

True. "Drop me off? No one will be the wiser."

Her calculating eyes study me. "Why do you need to do this?"

"To see if her home is haunted. Two accidents in two weeks *is* suspicious, and it's okay if you're scared, but she actually invited me to come over tonight, so technically, I don't think it's breaking and entering."

Helen Cross has never admitted to being scared of anything in her life. She draws herself up straighter and puffs out her chest. "Well, that does change the situation, doesn't it? Let me grab my handbag."

I NEVER EXPECTED my partner in crime to be my future mother-in-law.

Hannah's family home is situated on fifty acres of land northwest of town. With white fencing, horse stables, several barns, and a long sprawling drive lined with hundred-year-old oaks, the plantation house looks like a page from a history book. I wouldn't be surprised to see a woman in a hoop skirt on the sweeping veranda, replete with hanging baskets of ferns.

"It was a grand old place once," Helen muses as I return from opening the large gate and climb into her fancy car. A brief rain shower on our way here has left puddles on the asphalt. "The family goes back as many generations as yours and mine."

The summer days are long and the setting sun's rays roll over the lawn. Leftover drops of rain on the green grass glint peach and gold. I check my shoes for mud. They're wet but won't leave stains on the clean beige mat at my feet. "Still looks impressive to me."

She eases her gas guzzler down the lane. "Her father contracted out the farming, and Hannah continued to do the same for a year or so after he and her mother passed on. Then she started piece-mealing the place, selling off a chunk here and another there. The land, the horses, the equipment. Soon her family legacy was reduced to nothing but this meager estate, and the fortune gone. Selling peaches and boiled peanuts became the new industry. Such a waste."

Meager is in the eyes of the beholder. Between the house and grounds, it had to take a good deal of time, money, and upkeep. Plus, I knew she'd sold many of the assets to cover Sylvester's gambling debts. Helen probably did, too. "Did you know Hannah's husband?"

She follows the curving drive to the side of the house, rather than parking out front where the car can be seen from the road. "Grew up with him. Such a malcontent."

Scanning the area, I don't see any other vehicles. What I do see is the spirit of a girl with no shoes, a ragged dress, and corn-rows peeking at us from behind a giant maple. As we get out, she vanishes, and I grab my bag of supplies from the backseat. "He was a troublemaker growing up?"

Also checking for the presence of visitors, although the human variety, she turns in a circle to survey the area. "He was a juvenile delinquent by the age of thirteen. Always in trouble. Hannah was such a silly girl. Her parents forbade her from seeing him, but she would sneak out to do so. Eventually, his parents couldn't control him, and feared he'd end up in prison, so they sent him to a military school up north."

We walk to the veranda's side steps, two planters of marigolds and pansies overflowing the marble containers. "Did it help?"

"Not a wit." Her heels click on the porch as she marches for the door. She may have hidden her car from view, but she's not too worried about being seen, otherwise. Luckily, the closest neighbors are a mile away and the road has little traffic. "He only learned how to pretend he'd gotten his act together. Showed up back here in his smart uniform and spouting 'yes, ma'am' and 'no ma'am,' appearing for all intents and purposes as though he'd turned over a new leaf. Hannah fell for him all over again, and the next thing you know, she's pregnant."

"Pregnant?" She hadn't mentioned a child.

We skirt two rocking chairs with a table. In the center is an antique lantern with a candle inside. Three matching pots of herbs surround it. The front door has a welcome sign. Helen rings the doorbell. "Just to be safe," she says, as the deep *bing-bong* of the chime goes off, and then, "They had a baby girl. Sharon, I think her name was. She was in Charles' class. Left town the day she graduated."

The place is quiet. The massive walnut and glass door is locked. "Look under the lantern and the planters for a hidden key," I suggest. While she does that, I search the underside of the mat and back of the welcome sign.

We both come up empty-handed. "I'll go around to the rear. See if that entrance is unlocked."

"I'll check windows," she offers, and I realize I have seduced Logan's mother to the dark side.

A four-season porch runs the length of the back of the house, an outdoor kitchen with it. The screen squeaks when I try it. More chairs, a bigger table, and lots of pillows decorate the space, painted chickens on everything. In the corner is a TV hung from the ceiling, and houseplants galore.

The interior double doors are unlocked and lead to a mudroom and kitchen. Down the paneled hallway, I spot the ghost girl again. She keeps her head tilted down and stares at me from under bangs with large, brown eyes. "Hello?" I call to her.

Instantly, she vanishes.

On my way to the front, I pass dozens of rooms, most of the doors closed. Some are dark, the windows blocked with heavy curtains, and the furniture covered with white sheets, but I see no other spirits. I let Helen in, and start unpacking my supplies.

"What is all that?" she asks, scrunching up her nose.

"Hannah asked me to clear the energy of the house. Since she's remarrying, she wants to make sure this place doesn't have any negativity from the past hanging around."

"Uh huh." Helen is dubious. "You're evicting the you-knows."

"You can call them bananas, if it makes you feel better." It's a term Bis and I use in public when discussing spirits.

Her face screws up again. "What a curious term."

Better than 'you-knows.' "Yes, but it's easier to discuss around others." I pause, considering the young girl. I need to cross her over to be sure she makes it to the afterlife. Hard to do if she won't talk to me. "Can't hurt to clear the house, right?" I open a couple of windows and the humid evening air wraps around us.

"Are there bananas in *my* home?"

I wasn't expecting *that*. "Have you seen any?"

"Don't be ridiculous. I'm still not certain I believe in such things, but I am curious."

I light the smudge stick and blow out the flame, using a feather to distribute the smoke as I walk counterclockwise through the interior. She follows on my heels, and I know I need to answer her, but am worried how she'll take the truth. "Not in the house, but in the old barn that used to be the speakeasy? There are quite a few."

"Really?" She sounds bemused and I glance over my shoulder as we travel the hallway. One corner of her mouth is lifted. "How interesting. Have you spoken to any of them? Are they relatives?"

We enter what appears to be a formal living room. "I haven't delved into their backgrounds."

"I'd like to know more about them."

Now *that* is interesting. I finish with the room, blowing smoke into all the corners and around the windows. My bundle is going out since I didn't let it burn too long. I didn't want a repeat of what happened that morning with Hannah. "I suppose I can come out sometime and see if any of them will talk to me."

"Good."

Sounds like she's a believer to me. Over the next ten minutes, I finish smudging all the rooms, Helen drifting off to sit on the back porch. I say a prayer when I'm done and then I reach out to any ghosts who might be present and ask them to move on. I focus on forming a light-filled doorway and encourage the girl and Sylvester to walk into it.

Finally, I grab my invisible markers and head outside. The

sun has set and ambient light from the crescent moon is the only illumination. Helen returns inside to find a flashlight, determined to watch me write the sigils on the foundation of the house. I head for the north side to find a spot, and notice muddy footprints on the sidewalk. They are too big to be mine and resemble the bottom of a sneaker, rather than a dress shoe like my cohort wears.

When I check to see if they're fresh, my finger comes away muddy. The hair on the back of my neck rises and I stand to peer into the shadows. On this side, the murkiness is deeper and foreboding.

Someone has been here since it rained, but are they still present? If so, why haven't they made themselves known?

I drop into my crouch once more, pretending to be going back to my original job. My skin crawls with the idea that Sly's spirit is watching. More times than I care for, ghosts have attacked me when I've tried to force them to move on. Recently, by living folks as well. I reach in my bag for my pepper spray, and whisper to my guardian angel. "Persephone? Is Sly here?"

She doesn't respond nor make an appearance. The feeling I'm being watched subsides, though, so I go back to work.

I'm halfway through the first sigil when I hear Helen scream.

NINE

Pulse hammering, I race inside. I discover Helen in the kitchen, backed up against the range. Across from her is a woman close to my age, holding a pump action shotgun.

"Who are you and why are you in my house?" she demands.

Helen has her hands raised. Her face is as pale as her hair. "It's Sharon, correct? Don't you remember me? Helen Cross."

"Mrs. Cross?" The woman lowers the weapon a notch. "Chuck's mom?"

A smile of relief and Helen lowers her hands. "Yes, dear. It's me."

Sharon swings toward me when I enter the room, and my full hands go up, mimicking Helen's. "I'm Ava Fantome. Your mom is friends with mine."

The corner of her eyes narrow. "You're the mayor's daughter."

I nod. "Sorry about us barging in. We're worried about your mom and I was..." I have no idea if Sharon knows about the ghost of her dad or not. "I mean, we were..."

Helen comes to my rescue. "Your mother fell tonight at book club and is at the hospital. Ava and I are here to put together an overnight bag for her."

"She fell?" Sharon's arm drops like all the starch has gone out of her. "Again?"

I plunk my things on the table. "I'm afraid so. She went down some steps. We can give you a ride to see her if you like."

Sharon un-cocks the gun. Then she sets it in the corner and drops into a chair. "Is she okay?"

I sit as well. "You should call and see how's she doing. They'll be able to give you more details about the extent of her injuries."

"This is my fault," she says. "She's off her meds again. I know she is. I should have listened to my gut and marched in here yesterday and forced her to take her valium."

Helen and I exchange a look over Sharon's head. "She's on medication?" I ask gently.

Sharon nods and sniffs. "I work at a camp for kids in Arkansas and it's our busiest season, you know, with all the schools out and vacationers passing through. She started texting me last week, saying Daddy had finally come back and he was out to hurt her. She gets paranoid every time she quits her pills. Every. Time. This is the worst, though, in a long while. She kept saying he was going to hurt me, too. She was texting and calling me a dozen times a day to make sure I was okay. Of course, I was. I'm busy, Mom!"

Her voice rises with every sentence. As a daughter, I sympathize. "What did she mean that your dad had come back? He's deceased, right?"

"He died when I was eleven, but they never found the body, and for years, Mom was convinced it wasn't real. That he was going to show up out of nowhere and start the nightmare all over again." She uses a napkin to blow her nose and dab her eyes. "My family is so screwed up."

Helen fills a kettle and turns the stove on to heat the water. "All families have their difficulties."

Sharon scrunches up her nose. "What is that smell? Is something burning?"

"Just a bit of sage." I act as if this is a common thing. "Your mother asked me to smudge the place while I was here."

Her brows dip. "You one of those New Age folks?"

"Technically, smudging has been around for millennia, as have some of the other so-called *new* healing modalities. Many are actually quite ancient." Helen is now frowning, too. "Anyway, you were saying about your mom fearing your dad wasn't dead?"

She crumples the napkin. "Some nights after it happened, I'd stumble downstairs and find her sitting on a chair in the hall, keeping an eye on both doors." She points at the gun. "She'd have that loaded and in her lap. Freaked me out. I was just a kid, you know?"

We all look at the weapon, the image of Hannah on guard making me feel sorry for both of them. "Your father was violent, she told me. I'm sure it wasn't easy for her to feel safe, even with him gone."

"I used to hide in my closet when he went on a rampage. He never hurt me, but I was a coward. He always wanted a boy, and by the time I was out of diapers, he had me tossing footballs, changing the oil in his truck, even shooting." It explained her ease with the gun. "Used to have me hunt small game, rabbits and squirrels. I hated it. Hated *him*. I wanted some predator to go after him, see how he liked it. And then when he was killed, I was..." She hiccups and grabs a fresh napkin to dab at her eyes. "Relieved. That was my fault, too."

Helen locates cups and teabags and lines them up on the countertop. "How so?"

"I wished him dead." Sharon's bottom lip quivers. "Every time he made me practice shooting, or he beat her up, I wished him dead."

"Wishing doesn't make it so," I state. "Like you said, you were just a scared kid."

The kettle whistles. Helen pours the water. "When did your mother go on the medication?"

"Um." Sharon searches her memory. "I was a sophomore. She got pneumonia and when she was in the hospital, she started talking about Dad peering in the windows at her. The doctor did an evaluation and discovered the paranoia was out of hand. That's when he prescribed the pills."

"Did they help?" I ask.

"To an extent, yes." We each accept a cup of tea from Helen. Sharon thanks her, but sets it aside. "She's always so sure it's him. Man, even dead as a doorknob, he has his hooks in her. I finally took a few days of PTO so I could come home and follow her around. See if she was acting crazier than normal because of her tumble last week. I know it sounds terrible that I didn't inform her I was here, but if she knew I was looking for proof she needs more meds, she'd try to cover it up. I suppose that makes me a bad daughter."

"It only makes you a concerned one," Helen cajoles, sipping her drink. "There's no shame in that. She's lucky to have you."

Sharon wrings her fingers. "But if I'd been forthright with her, maybe her accident tonight wouldn't have happened. I should have at least told Burt."

I've forgotten about him. "Can you notify him regarding your mother's fall? I'm not sure anyone has."

"I still can't believe he would marry her." She blanches and looks down. "Sorry, that was unkind. She's just so…"

I pat her arm. "It's okay. We understand."

As if we've conjured him, a man appears. "Sharon?"

She jumps, her hand knocking against the table and spilling her tea. "Burt? What are you doing here?"

Burt Dietmar is of average height, a few extra pounds around his middle, and wearing khaki slacks and a knit shirt with a designer logo on it. "I'm supposed to meet your mother. She didn't tell me you were visiting."

"Hannah fell at book club tonight," I inform him, hoping to divert any awkwardness. I come to my feet and offer a hand. "I'm Ava Fantome, and this is Helen Cross."

"Helen," he nods to her and I realize they know each other. "Is Hannah okay? Is she upstairs?"

Helen sets her cup in the sink. "She's in the hospital, Burt. We don't know the extent of her injuries yet, but she was conscious and speaking before the ambulance arrived."

Tears slip from Sharon's eyes. "I'm really worried about her."

Burt puts his hands on his hips. "Lordy, I had no idea. Why didn't someone call me?"

"I didn't have your number," I say. "And we should get out of your hair so you can check on her." I turn to Sharon. "Can we give you a lift?"

"I'll take her," Burt insists.

He moves to stand at her side and it hits me like a two-ton brick. They share the same eyebrows, the same dimple in the center of their chins.

Oh boy.

Ghosts know a lot of things. My friend, Winter, claims some know all. If, since passing on, Sly discovered Sharon's true parentage, it could be motive to hang around the earthly plain and take revenge on Hannah.

But why now? Why not twenty years ago?

Why hasn't he done anything against Burt?

Rubbing her eyes, Sharon blows out an audible breath. "Thank you. I just need to pull myself together before we go."

Helen and I exit the house. In the car, Helen flips on the headlights and the beams bounce on the tree trunks lining the drive as we leave. I see no ghosts, and I hope I've helped at least one soul tonight.

"Strange that Hannah couldn't let herself believe Sylvester was good and truly dead," Helen comments on the way into town.

"I suppose when you haven't seen the body, the possibility lingers in the back of your mind." I fiddle with my engagement ring. All this with Hannah and Sharon is weighing heavy on me. I don't doubt Hannah believes Sly is haunting her, but is he? Her mental state in question, I have to look at this with a different perspective. "How well do you know Burt?"

"He's a member of the Club."

Which tells me nothing outside of the fact he has money. "Have you known him long?"

"This is Thornhollow. I've known him since grade school, but we didn't run in the same circles. Still don't. We see each other in passing, and at Club events. Why?"

"Just curious. It's probably good that Hannah has him."

She offers nothing else, and every fishing question I formulate about him and Hannah could put the bloodhound onto the fact Sharon is Burt's daughter. Helen is shrewd and probably already knows, although I'd expect her to gossip about it. Quite possibly the whole town knows, but in case they don't, I refuse to be the one to air Hannah's secrets.

Logan is on the couch, reading one of his law journals, when we arrive. It's late, I'm tired, but seeing him lifts my mood. His sleeves are rolled to his elbows and he's holding a whiskey glass in his other hand. As I enter, he glances up and smiles. "Hello, sweetheart."

He's wearing a pair of sexy reading glasses, having removed his contacts. When Helen crosses the threshold behind me, the smile falters, and he sets down the magazine and drink. "Mother?" He shoots to his feet and looks to me once more. "Is everything okay?"

"Other than you haven't returned my call in two days?" She whisks past me to accept his kiss. "Yes."

"Mostly," I tell him. I didn't get to finish the sigils on Hannah's house, but with her in the hospital at the moment, it's unnecessary. Sharon didn't mention anything about ghosts, and I'll go back once Hannah is home. I'd prefer not to end up with buckshot in me. "We're fine, but there was an incident at book club. Hannah Grady fell down the stairs. She's in the hospital. Your mother was gracious enough to visit Hannah's daughter with me to break the news."

"I won't stay long," Helen says, glancing at her watch. "But I do need to speak to you."

I head for the kitchen. "Wine, Helen?"

"No, thank you," she responds. I hear her say to Logan, "Is there a reason you haven't returned my call?"

"Sorry?"

"I got your voicemail when I phoned. I requested for you to get back to me. It's so unlike you, Logan."

When I return with my glass of white, one of the best varieties from her vineyard, Logan is scrolling through his call records. "There's no call or message from you."

"Hmm." It's amazing how much she can convey with that one tiny sound. Perplexed at how such a thing could happen, suspicious he's deleted them on purpose, and annoyed either way. The only thing it doesn't express is the possibility she didn't actually call him. "How odd."

"Technology is great when it works properly." I take a sip and feel the cool liquid trickle down my throat. Spending that much time with her wasn't horrible, but guarding every word for fear I'd say something wrong was tedious, not to mention keeping myself from blurting out the news about the secret wedding. "But it stinks when it doesn't."

Logan gives his mom a big smile. The one that gets him off the hook with me anytime I'm upset. No surprise, since he's practiced it on her thousands of times and she reacts the way I always do. Her lips lift because she can't help but give in, and she waves the issue away. "I'm here now, so we can discuss it."

"What is *it*?" he asks.

I raise my glass, as if in toast. "We're throwing Chuck and Trysta an engagement party."

Logan's brows shoot up and the smile falls off his face. "Awesome," he replies, recovering quickly, but he picks up the whiskey glass and downs the last of the contents.

TEN

The next morning, I have two people to visit at the hospital.

Hannah is sitting up, and although her nose is swollen and there's a nasty bruise on her collarbone, she seems in good spirits. We discuss what happened, but I can tell she's fuzzy on the details. I'm not sure if it's from the after effects of the accident, or the medications they're pumping into her veins.

"He was there," she insists.

"Sly?"

Her hair is matted from sleep. "I know you think I'm looney. Maybe I am. I heard a noise down there, and when I went to check it out, I saw a face in the window across from the restroom. Next thing I know, *bam*. Someone pushed me."

"A face? Like a reflection?"

Her gaze drops and she toys with the edge of the blanket where it's fraying. "Ghosts can float, right? It was him, I swear." She folds a section of the material over and smooths it with trembling hands. "Sharon thinks I've lost it. I'm totally cuckoo. Maybe she's correct."

Logan and I stayed up late, discussing the party, Hannah and her ghost, and our wedding situation—or non-situation, as it happens to be at the moment. I did a search on Sylvester and found nothing that suggested he was alive. Yet, I can't shake the feeling that if he *is* a ghost, I have to use other tactics on him, like I'm doing with Trysta. "I've asked my father to do an in-depth background check on Sylvester. His family, his friends, his old contacts. Even the coroner's report and the police officers who were at the scene of his death."

Her eyes widen. "Why?"

"It will ease my mind,"—*and yours*—"if I confirm he died that day in the woods."

She leans forward and I see her throat move as she swallows. "You think he's still...?"

"No, but reviewing the facts may turn up something I can use to encourage his spirit to move on." *And hopefully, help you move on, too.*

Her head, flat hair and all, bobs and she sinks back against the pillow. "I love that idea."

"I'd also like to, with your permission, set up security cameras at your house, as a safety measure. I may be able to catch the ghost on camera."

Her eyes light. "You can do that?"

"I have a friend who can." *I hope.*

"Yes, by all means. Anything to prove I'm not losing the last of my marbles."

I leave her and head to Gloria's room. Her face is bathed in sunlight from the window, but she is, all the same, still pale and withdrawn. At least today, she is awake and accepts my hug. "You've had a rough time," I say, pulling up the nearby chair.

"I feel so helpless." Her voice is weak, rough. There is a cup of ice chips on the tray next to her and she fumbles to get one out. "I just want to go home."

I help with the ice. "When are they releasing you?"

Sucking on the piece, her frail shoulders lift in what passes as a shrug. "My blood tests don't show any cause for it. Stool sample is normal. The doctor is at a loss, and now they aren't sure it was food poisoning. They want to keep me for more tests."

An invisible cause...like some kind of magic, perhaps? "Did you happen to eat anything from the new bakery?"

A crease appears between her brows. "It's not open yet, is it?"

"No, but Trysta has been delivering samples all over town."

"Oh." Her eyes clear a bit. "Is that where the chocolate caramel cupcakes came from?"

"You ate one?"

Again, a slight shrug. "I believe Brynlee brought them. I thought she'd made them and didn't realize they were from the bakery. Delicious, that's for sure."

"Did Joseph or Brynlee eat them? Any of the seamstresses?"

"I assume they did. We were so busy that day, though, and they can be sneaky." She chuckles weakly. "They know the rules about having food at their workstations. We can't have fingerprints or stains on the gowns."

Yet, they were all at work yesterday when I was there. I'm stumped.

Unless... "Have you met Trysta?"

"Just in passing. She waved at me last week when I left your place on Wednesday after the dress fittings."

I mentally curse. Is she going after people I care about? Even if she is, I have no proof, and no one who can help me force her to move on. It's all on me.

"Which reminds me, I may not be able to do fittings this

week." She sighs. "Regan can take my place. Call Joseph and tell him to send her."

I do as she requests and secure the seamstress to handle our Wednesday brides. "Hey, Joseph? Did you eat any of the cupcakes the other day?"

"What cupcakes? There were cupcakes?" He sounds a bit miffed. "No one told me."

"Gloria thinks Brynlee brought them in. You didn't see any?"

He hollers into the room, "Did Brynlee bring cupcakes?" I can't hear the responses but a moment later, he says to me, "Nobody has brought any this week, doll. She must be confused."

"Okay, thank you." After I disconnect, I inform her Regan is taking care of the fittings, and she sinks deeper into her pillow.

"That's good." I see her chewing something over in her mind. "Why would you think the treats caused this?"

"It was something your nurse mentioned yesterday about viruses and bacteria showing up in everything these days."

She's too weak to pursue it. Staying a while longer, I try to get her talking about the fall/winter wedding season, which she loves. She apologizes for my dress and I assure her it's no big deal. "At this point, I'm not sure we're going through with the vows anyway."

She reaches out a shaky hand and I take it. "Oh, Ava, you wish to marry in the summer surrounded by Willa's beautiful garden."

"Absolutely, but I can't go behind Helen's back."

Her grasp is firmer than I expect as she squeezes my fingers. "So invite her."

"She won't come and she will make my life miserable,

Logan's, too, if we say our vows before her October shindig. That's her dream."

"You are stuck between a rock and a very big hard place."

"I am at that."

"Sometimes, we have to do what's best for us, and let the consequences fall where they may. All you can do is be honest with her, and tell her your plan, then let her decide how to react. That's not on you. If she wants to be part of the summer wedding, then she'll swallow her pride and attend. If not, so be it."

Gradually, I change the subject, and she seems to have more energy by the time I leave. Back at The Wedding Chapel, I find Jenn sorting through the day's appointment book. "Hey," she says when I walk in. She's in black from head to toe and has her hair up in a simple ponytail. "Before you ask why I'm working, Penn is watching Yasmine and I need a few hours of adult interaction. This being a mom thing is harder than I expected."

Being a daughter is no picnic either. "It's good to see you. I'm glad you're here."

"You are?"

"Have you ever planned an engagement party?"

She grins and Rosie snorts from across the room, having already heard about the one I'm now in charge of. "I'm a fast learner," Jenn assures me.

Relieved she's willing, I put her to work on securing a location and coming up with three different themes for Helen to choose from.

Meanwhile, the new security system has racked up dozens of clips. I sit to review them, excited at first, then growing bored as video after video is of birds, a wasp determined to build a nest on the camera, a neighborhood raccoon, two stray cats, and an opossum who all strolled by the previous night. Not one of them is of Trysta, Sam, Aunt Willa or any other ghost, but the sensitivity of the motion sensor is extremely high.

I call Sage. "Sorry," she says, not sounding remorseful at all, "that's how a motion detector works. The only way to adjust it is to make the cameras run constantly."

Which would be *hours* of footage. No thanks. "Can I hire you to set up a similar system at a client's house?"

"Are you looking for human, supernatural, or both?"

"Let's start with both."

"Is this situation tied in with yours?

I doodle on my calendar. "No, but I'm not sure what I'm dealing with. Could be they're imagining things."

"People tend to see ghosts where there aren't any. When and where?"

I rattle off the address. "Let's shoot for installing it tomorrow. Hannah should be home from the hospital by then. I'll make an appointment with her and text you the time."

"After three. I have a shift at the shop."

My mind flashes back to Daddy and his weed extermination. "What if we remove the cords from the men? Yank them out like a weed, roots and all, so they can't grow back?"

There is a pause as she seems to consider it. "It can be done, but it takes an advanced practitioner and permission from those involved."

"Surely, I can get the ghosts to grant me permission."

"*All* those involved, including Trysta. You could also remove the cords from her end, severing the connection to them that way."

I sit up straighter. "That would free the men?"

"The cords would dissolve on their own since they're no longer attached to a recipient. Like a dead electrical wire."

"How do I do it? Please tell me I don't need her permission."

"It won't work otherwise. And you need someone with experience for that type of thing. It's heavy duty energy work and requires a delicate but forceful touch."

Can I trick Trysta into giving me permission? I'm not sure that's ethical, but what she's doing is a far cry from it as well. I need to convince her to stop tormenting those men and head to the afterlife. Fat chance of that. "But you know how, right?"

"Understanding how it works and having experience doing it are two different things."

Heaviness weighs on my shoulders. "I understand. I'll be in touch."

I know some very experienced witches who perform healings. Can't hurt to call on Winter and see what she and her sisters recommend. First, I text Daddy and request he switch gears to look into Sly's supposed death.

"The Country Club is available June twenty-first," Jenn announces, waltzing to my desk. She's lost most of her baby weight but her cheeks are still round and her dimple is deeper when she grins. "It actually wasn't until I worked my magic." She makes a starburst gesture with her hand. "But only in the evening, and if I don't book it today, that slot will be gone."

"Do it." Unless I figure out how to stop Trysta soon, and not end up behind prison bars doing it, I have no option but to proceed as if everything is normal. With this ghost, I'm playing a long game and I have to act as if I'm happy to welcome her to the family. "Put it in Helen's name, but inform them it's a surprise and they're to keep it hush-hush."

"You got it." She twirls away, seemingly happy to be *working her magic.*

Happy employees make me happy, too. "Good to have you back," I call after her.

Rosie smiles from across the way. "Ready for our two o'clock?"

My stomach growls as I check the time. "I'll grab a bite of food and be right back."

In the kitchen, I warm leftovers and start to message Winter. As I'm composing it, she actually texts me. *What's wrong? Persephone says you're in over your head with this situation.*

The angel is a step ahead of me. *Hate to admit it, but she's right.*

How can I help?

That's my friend. She sees ghosts, too, and is always ready to lend a hand when I'm dealing with a difficult one. *Can I call you tonight?*

Looking forward to it. Do we need Mama Nightengale for this one?

I have no idea, but I love Winter's friend. She has a lot of spunk, and I dig her bird. *If she's available.*

The rest of the afternoon flies by. I see how it taxes Rosie and I'm doubly glad Jenn is back, even if it's only a few hours here and there. Before she leaves for the day, the three of us discuss her resuming her regular part-time status in the coming weeks. I don't consider myself psychic, but I have the feeling Rosie is going to deliver early.

With those plans made, I send them home and sit to do paperwork. Logan emerges from his office a while later and we finish the leftovers and share our respective days. "At least you've managed to keep Trysta from barging in announced," he says, as he pushes aside an empty plate.

I'm about to raise my wine glass in salute when the back door bangs open. "Anyone home?" a familiar voice calls.

We're both tired and it's late. "Now, if I could just figure out how to keep the rest of the world out," I grumble.

Brax and Rhys enter the kitchen a moment later, bringing

dessert. My grumpiness morphs into joy at the speed of light when I see the chocolate cheesecake and caramel ice cream.

"You know you love us," Rhys says, setting the delicious treat in front of me and going for plates. He's already in his pajamas, while Brax wears a smart looking suit.

Logan winks at me and Brax opens a drawer to pull out the scoop. "And bonus, guys and dolls, it's not from that deadly bakery across the street."

"Thank you," I say. I haven't told them everything, but enough that they know Killer Cupcakes may indeed be deadly.

Within moments, we all have servings of yumminess in front of us. "First, the wedding," Rhys says around a mouthful. "Are we still on for Friday morning?"

"About that." Logan swallows a scoop of ice cream and then tells them about our mutual cold feet.

They sympathize and we eat more sugar. Then Brax wipes his hands and tosses his napkin away. "Now for the ugly stuff."

I don't like the sound of that. "Are you guys okay?"

"We're fine," Rhys tells me with a pat on the hand. "It's you and your ghost friend we're worried about."

Logan gets up and snags the bourbon. He pours all of us a glass. "Ava's working on it. Trysta's case is an unusual one."

Rhys waves a hand in the air. "Not that spirit. Although, we're here for you, if you need our help, of course."

Now I'm really wary. "What are you talking about?"

They exchange a glance and Brax frowns at me. "You don't know?"

I shake my head. "Know what?"

"The B&B has a ghost problem," Rhys tells me. "And he goes by the name of Sherlock."

ELEVEN

S herlock showed up last fall when I was working on the case involving Logan's family curse.

I sip the bourbon at the revelation he's haunting the house next door. "I wondered where he'd gone off to, but I assumed he was doing his usual and hanging out at the Magical Library of Witches and Wizards, where I first met him. Are he and Persephone fighting again?"

Brax shrugs. "We were hoping you could tell us."

Logan rises and clears the plates. "How do you know it's him? Can you see him?"

"No, and thank heaven for that," Brax utters. "But weird things have been happening."

Rhys nods emphatically. "An entity keeps pulling out my Sherlock Holmes' collection and leaving the volumes all over the house. They're rare, signed editions. I don't let anyone touch them."

I learn something new about my friends every day. "I didn't know you were a Holmes fan."

"I gave him the set at Christmas," Brax says. "Leo Kingsley, that vintage book broker I know, had them for sale. They are pretty rare, and Rhys is extremely careful with them."

Rhys slams back his bourbon in one shot. "The other day, I was telling a guest about my orchids and that I'd misplaced the fertilizer for them. I heard a man's voice in my ear, 'Deductive reasoning is your friend. You might use it. Check the shed.' Freaked me right out! There was no one else there. I asked the guest if she was a ventriloquist, throwing her voice like that and sounding like a man, and she thought I'd lost my marbles. Later, I went to the shed and there it was. The box of fertilizer was right in the center of the bench."

I see Logan trying to hide a smirk. "Could be coincidence."

"It was *not*." Rhys looks miffed. "When Brax called tonight to let me know he was coming home, I asked him to pick up a cheese-cake from his mama's place. I heard that same voice again and it said to add the ice cream because, and I quote, 'Ava needs it.'"

Sherlock knows I have a weakness for the stuff. "That's kind of sweet. No pun intended," I add.

Rhys rolls his eyes. "He did the line."

"The line?" Logan asks.

"'It's elementary, dear Watson.'" Brax supplies.

"That's what he said to me." Rhys glances around as if he believes our detective ghost is eavesdropping. "You would tell me if he were here, right?"

I assure him the place is clear. "I will talk to him."

"Why is he haunting us?" Rhys asks.

I wouldn't call what they've described haunting in the strictest terms. Sherlock believes he's being helpful, not scary. "He likes you, is all. He's not trying to frighten you."

"Well, he needs to move back over here."

"Persephone?" I call. My angel is silent. I shrug. "Sherlock?"

Nothing happens.

Logan loads the dishwasher. "You used to think it would be cool to have a resident spirit," Logan teases.

"That's before it actually happened." Rhys shivers and glances at me. "Help?"

I pat his hand. "I'll come over first thing tomorrow and speak with him, okay?"

He throws his arms around my neck. "Thank you."

After they leave, Logan massages my shoulders. "Want me to draw you a bath?"

"That sounds like heaven." My stomach is full and my body relaxed from the sugar rush and bourbon. "First, I have to talk to Winter. Raincheck?"

He kisses my cheek. "You know where to find me."

In my room, I establish a video chat with my friend. Mamma N is with her and they wave at me onscreen. The parrot sticks his face in front of the camera and I get a close up of his eye before his owner pulls him away. "Sorry about that," Mamma Nightengale says. "Naughty bird."

Winter's dark hair is piled high on her head, the single silvery streak in the mix looking like snow. Mamma N is dressed in a flamboyant orange kaftan I bet Persephone would love.

I tell them what's going on with Trysta, and the option of cord removal, watching Winter's face grow serious, and Mamma N looks slightly horrified. While her mother and grandmother practiced Voodoo, she's into white magic only, and is as much a novice to some of this stuff as I am.

"We need Summer." Winter gets up. "I'll be right back."

As she goes to find her sister, Mamma N tsks. "Girl, you are always finding trouble. Can't you mix up a potion or something to make this gal go away?"

I'm not a witch, although Tabby is, and her blood runs through me. "I wish it were that easy."

Winter returns with her younger sister in tow. "Hi, Ava." Summer is blond and freckled-face, glowing like a sunny day. "Winter said you need help with energy transfer."

I explain the situation once more, watching her bright disposition darken. When I'm done, she purses her lips and writes notes on a slip of paper she's brought with her. "I'm going out on a limb here, but guessing this ghost won't take kindly to you trying to unhitch her batteries. Like your friend Sage told you, you need an experienced energy worker to do it."

"Or some powerful witchcraft," Mamma Nightengale adds, nodding.

Winter, standing over them and staring down at the camera, asks, "What if we used both?" They glance up, questioning, and she continues. "Witchcraft to make her compliant. Energy work to free the ghosts."

Summer brightens once more. "I like how you think, sister."

"Sounds promising." I pull out my own pad and pen. "How exactly, though? Do I have to use a spell?"

"Are the men still alive?" Mamma N asks. "If not, can't Ava simply burn their bones? Or I know!" She claps her chubby hands. "She can burn *Trysta's*. She's dead, right? If you burn what's left of her to ash, that will eliminate the whole problem."

Winter places a hand on the woman's shoulder. "That's certainly what she deserves, but her spirit will still be hanging around. She'll be even less likely to cross if we piss her off, and we really do need her to move across the veil."

We sure do. "I don't need an angry ghost haunting me the rest of my life."

Summer laughs. "I wouldn't wish that on anyone."

"But if I use a spell to incapacitate her for the cord removal, that's not getting her permission." Sage was adamant about that. "Don't I need her to be agreeable to what we're doing for it to work?"

"See, here's the thing with energy work," Summer says, "I assume she took the men's life force without their permission, which violates the rules around free will. While she may or may not practice the Craft, the law is clear. What harm you do comes back three-fold. It would be ideal to have her compliance to remove the cords, but in essence, she's wronged these spirits, so she doesn't get a say in it. You're rescuing them, and keeping further harm from being done. The only issue I see is that she'll be a true ghost once you sever the ties, and you'll have the same issue—she may be less than happy about it."

May be? She'll hate me and most likely want my head on a chopping block. "Why do ghosts have to be so difficult?"

Winter gives a knowing laugh. "Ain't that the truth? Let me do more research on what type of spell to use and I'll get back to you. Meantime, see if you can figure out what motivates her to stay earthbound in her physical form. She's gone to extreme lengths for it, way more than the average person would ever consider. Understanding her motivation could help."

"Wait!" Mamma Nightengale snaps her fingers. "If she's using magic, she might have organic matter from each of those poor men, and she has to keep it close to keep sucking on their energy. It acts as a conduit between them."

Summer and Winter nod in unison. "That's a possibility," Winter says.

I'm afraid to ask. "Organic matter...?"

"Fingernails, hair, that sort of thing," Summer explains. "If she used magic to create a binding spell, destroying the ingredients of it could cut her ties to them."

"That would be a whole lot easier than casting a spell on her and yanking out the cords," Mamma N says.

Hunting the organic matter down is no piece of cake. She's

probably hidden it well, if that's what she's using. "True, but I *still* end up with an angry ghost on my hands."

We all go quiet, thinking it over. Summer sighs. "Perhaps once she doesn't have a physical form to inhabit, she'll decide staying here isn't that great and move on."

It's unlikely, but her positive outlook is better than mine. "I appreciate all of you. I'll see what I can uncover about her motivations."

We say goodnight, then I sit and stew, writing different ideas down. I hear the water in the bathroom running and when I finally drag myself to change into my sleep shirt, a warm bath is waiting for me. There are even bubbles.

"Enjoy," is all Logan says before he disappears downstairs, heading back to work.

This man. I so love him. I shed my clothes, sink into the water, and close my eyes. I try to forget about ghosts, sick friends, and the items on my never-ending to-do list.

Five minutes into it, I'm warm, my muscles are relaxed, and my skin is beginning to get pruny, and then...my guardian angel pops in. "What do you want?" she asks.

I jerk, sending the fading bubbles in all directions, and my eyes fly open. "Does no one knock anymore? Yeesh."

"You called." She's sitting on the closed toilet seat lid in a turquoise dress with gold embroidered flowers all over it. Her matching earrings fall to her shoulders and it appears she's cleaned out the makeup counter at the local Walgreens. "I'm here. What is it?"

A few hours late, but okay. I pull the last of the bubbles toward me, my skin suddenly cool and pebbling with goosebumps. "Are you fighting with Sherlock again?"

Her eye roll is Emmy worthy. "Why do you care about him?"

"I care about both of you." My towel is out of reach. I'm

sure the angel has seen her share of naked people, yet I can't bring myself to stand and flash her in order to snag it. "He's hanging around at the B&B, and my friends are less ghost tolerant than I am. Can you talk to him and ask him to not talk to Rhys or mess with his stuff?"

"You want me to lay down the law to him?" She grins. "Why didn't you say so?"

"Don't—" *make him mad*, I'm about to say, but she's already gone. "Great."

I pull the plug and the water swirls. The towel is soft and I wrap myself in it, longing for my bed and sleep. I make it to my room a few minutes later, ready to crash, when Sherlock himself pays me a visit with no warning.

"You hate me, don't you?" He floats toward the bed, where I've only just tucked the covers around me.

Tabby is already bedded down and yawns at him. I sigh. "First of all, of course I don't. I'm quite fond of you. Secondly, you're invading my privacy, and this can wait until tomorrow."

He pushes his glasses up his nose. "You sent that...that angel after me."

The way he snarls the word makes it sound like Persephone is a horrible disease. "I only wanted her to ask you not to hang out at the B&B. You're frightening my friends."

This seems to surprise him. "But they know me."

"They know you help me, and they're cool with that, but when a disembodied voice starts speaking to you, it's unnerving. They can't see you like I can, and they don't feel comfortable with you in their house."

"This is preposterous."

"Did Samuel talk to you about watching out for my friend, Hannah?"

"We've discussed the situation and I went by her home. There is no ghost of her husband there."

Interesting. "I didn't sense him either. He must be a slippery one."

He shrugs, still miffed about my request to leave Rhys and Brax alone.

"Why are you visiting the B&B so much? What did Persephone do this time?"

He drifts to the window overlooking the backyard. "This is not about her. I know when I'm not wanted."

Before I can argue, he vanishes.

Ghosts. I flop down on my pillow. *What a pain.*

TWELVE

The next morning I text Rhys and tell him I spoke to Sherlock and he shouldn't have any more issues.

He's relieved, but asks if he's angered the ghost. I assure him Sherlock is fine, even though he's not.

I wish I could smooth things over with him, but the only way to do that would be to play matchmaker, or perhaps psychiatrist, to him and Persephone. I don't have time, nor am I the best person for that job, because what do I know about ghosts and angels when it comes to romance?

I plan to have a long talk with Persephone, though. I know she's enamored with him, and he with her. This back and forth, on again-off again romance has to stop. The drama is wearing me out.

The hospital phones during breakfast to let me know Gloria is being released. I kiss Logan and rush out, messaging Rosie as I get in the car. *Picking up Gloria. Be back soon.*

Hopefully before our first bride arrives for her fitting. Regan should be here by then and Rosie assures me she can get her set up and handle the client.

Before I see Gloria, I check on Hannah and discover she's already gone home. I call her house and Burt answers. "She's fine," he tells me when I ask.

"That's great. May I speak with her?"

"She's resting."

His tone is clipped, as if he's annoyed about my concern. "Can you have her contact me when she's up and about? We have some items to discuss."

"About what?"

I can't tell him it's in regard to catching Sly on camera. "About her birthday party."

"Party? She didn't tell me anything about that."

"We haven't locked anything in yet, what with your upcoming nuptials and all. Please just have her call me."

I pray Hannah will understand.

Gloria is in a wheelchair, ready to be escorted out, when I arrive at her room. Her release papers and handbag rest in her lap. "Ava, I'm so glad to see you."

Her color is normal and her eyes clear. I lean down and give her a hug. "Ditto, my friend. I was worried about you."

"I don't need this chair," she states emphatically. "But they insist I have to stay in it until I get through the front doors."

An orderly enters. "Hospital policy, Miss Gloria. Dr. Ernestine will have my hide if we don't treat you properly." He winks at me. "Consider yourself a queen who is being pampered by her loyal subjects."

She warms to the attention, which is also nice to see. He walks us to my waiting car and assists Gloria into it. She continues to act irritated at the kid-glove treatment, but settles once we're on our way.

I take the turn to head out of town but she argues with me. "I want to go to The Wedding Chapel. I have things to do."

"You just got out of the hospital. You need rest."

"I've been in bed for two solid days. I need to join the living again. If you don't take me with you, I'll simply work at my place."

Letting her come home with me isn't the best idea, but her stubbornness is insurmountable. I've tested it before. "On one condition."

She sits straighter. "Name it, *cherie*."

Her native French comes out when she's emotional. This means a lot to her. I consider how wise this is, but bottom line, if she's at my house, I can keep an eye on her. If I take her to hers, she'll rush over to Miss Jasmine's before I back out of the parking lot.

Joseph cares for her, but he'll be so tied up with orders and sales, he won't pay close attention to her and she'll end up overdoing it. "It's fitting day and Regan is already sched-uled to take your spot. You can hang out and assist her, but you have to take lots of breaks and sit on the sofa as much as you stand up. I will not have you taking over and taxing yourself."

She purses her lips and I anticipate where the negotiation is headed. Then she draws a deep breath and nods sharply. "Fine."

Wow, that was easy. *Take the win*, I tell myself. "Promise?"

The corners of her eyes narrow and she deflates. "You got me."

Aha. That's why it was so easy. She didn't intend to follow my compromises if I didn't force a pledge out of her. I arch an eyebrow at her. "I can and will hogtie you to a chair."

She pokes my side, making me laugh. "You'll do no such thing. I promise, okay?"

Still smiling, I pull into traffic, heading for home. "Did you have breakfast?"

"If you can call that awful, bland gruel they serve a meal."

"How about we stop at The Beehive and get you some decent southern food?"

"*Oui*."

Speaking of food. "Did they ever determine for sure what caused your illness?"

"Dr. Ernestine still believes it's food poisoning. She wants me to stick to the BRAT diet—bananas, rice, applesauce, toast—but I'm starving. And I don't care for bananas."

My mind thinks of Helen and the code for ghosts. "Toast and applesauce it is," I say, and against her arguments of needing eggs, sausage, and a blueberry muffin, that's exactly what I get her.

Regan is present and working on Delaney Morand's dress when we arrive. I put Gloria on the sofa with a TV tray and her food, and greet the bride who's chosen my most popular ball-gown to marry in. Jenn shows up halfway through the fitting and *oohs* and *ahhs* over it, making Delaney beam.

Hannah calls a bit later, seeming confused about the birthday party reference. "Did I tell you I was turning fifty?"

"Mama did. That's not why I wanted to speak to you. Remember our discussion about installing cameras at your place to see if we pick up paranormal activity?" Or any *not* so paranormal. "I was hoping my friend and I could come by later this afternoon."

The line is quiet for a long moment. "Did your dad find anything?"

I'm guessing not since he hasn't called me. "Not yet. Are you still good with us putting up the cameras?"

Her voice grows quiet, barely above a whisper. "I think Sharon and Burt are suspicious."

"Of what?"

"That I'm telling the truth. They've chalked all this off to my imagination, but something happened while I was gone. I can tell. They're both acting odd."

Could be even more reason to have hidden cameras in place. "Perhaps it would be best if we install the system when they're gone."

"I was thinking the same. Sharon is leaving this afternoon—that girl can't get out of here soon enough. She hates this house. Burt will be golfing at five. Will that work?"

"Let's plan on it. If anything comes up, call me, okay?"

We disconnect.

My afternoon is full of fittings and keeping Gloria from overdoing it, which is not as hard as I'd anticipated, but still challenging. Her love for the dresses is evident, and while Regan is an accomplished seamstress, Gloria has an emotional connection with every bride she measures and tucks. More than once, Rosie and I exchange knowing smiles when Gloria adjusts Regan's workmanship in the midst of keeping the client gushing about her upcoming event.

The Quiggs stop by with a contractor to take a look at the homestead's roof. It is long past due for shingles and until the leaks are fixed, the interior work is on hold.

My appointment reminder dings at ten minutes before three to jog my memory that Ophelia is coming to discuss her internship. I'm knee-deep in video clips while I chat with one of my suppliers for party decorations, lining up what we'll need for the engagement shindig. Helen has informed me she likes the Golden Era, black and gold theme out of the three Jenn came up with. It feels like a waste of time and energy, but I have to keep up the appearance of planning it.

The teen girl is barely five feet tall, with a round face, dozens of corkscrew curls cut just below her ears, and heavy, purple framed glasses. "This is so cool," she says, as way of introduction when she arrives. Her almond shaped eyes take in the details of the display windows, my office, and Rosie's belly.

"Welcome, Ophelia." I shake her hand and motion her to the chair across from me. "My office manager is Rosie,"—I point to her—"and I'm Ava."

"Oh, I know," she says, bobbing her head as she removes her crossbody bag and plops down. "You're the medium."

Guess I need to get that out of the way before we get down to business. "I have a few skills in that area, but I'm more interested in you. Tell me about yourself."

"You can call me Lia—only my mom calls me by my full name, and that's usually when she's upset at me." She grins and pushes her glasses up her nose. "Anyway, I'm a ghost hunter."

I blink away my surprise, my smile faltering. "I thought you were a bookkeeping intern."

"Oh yeah. That, too." More head bobbing, the corkscrews flying. "I'll get you all set up, no problem. Are there any ghosts here right now?"

I hold back a sigh. Tabby moseys in and rubs her orange marmalade body against Lia's leg.

The girl jumps, then seeing it's a cat and not a ghost, reaches down and picks her up. "I love cats! She's so pretty."

Tabby rubs her head against Lia's hand. "We have several of them and a dog in residence," I inform her. "I hope that won't bother you."

"Not at all. The more, the merrier."

Rosie brings over a clipboard that she hands to Lia. "We have an accounting system, but need something that's easier and less time consuming. Could you fill this out for me?"

Our 'system,' as such, is a basic spreadsheet. No bells or whistles, but her description sounds more professional.

The girl reaches for it and Tabby jumps down. "Um, sure. Then can I check for ghosts?"

"Check, how?" Rosie glances at me.

I shake my head. *Do not encourage her.*

Fumbling with her bag while trying to hang onto the clipboard, Lia drops it, and Tabby scatters. "I brought my EMF detector and ghost box."

"A box?" I'm curious enough to peer over the desk to see what she's digging for.

"What does it do?" Rosie also scrutinizes her.

Retrieving the fallen board, Lia huffs at her clumsiness and a necklace falls loose from where she's tucked it inside her shirt. It swings in the sunlight, the glass vial pendant bouncing the light from the display window around the room.

Persephone pops in and points to it. "Pay attention."

"I made it myself." Lia secures the clipboard on her lap, then gently teases out a black box from her purse. "It sweeps radio channels to create a white noise effect and picks up spirits if they talk. Do you want to see it in action?"

I don't need to. I see where she gets at least some of her looks when her grandfather, a short man with gray hair and glasses, is suddenly beside her. The teddy bear on the shelf beeps wildly and Rosie flinches, covering her ears. "Oh, jeez."

The spirit smiles down on his granddaughter's head. "She's quite the engineer," he tells me, his spectral body hovering in the air. "I'm so proud of her."

"Do you have an EMF, too?" Lia asks, looking at the bear.

My attention lands on the necklace and I get up to switch the equipment off. Returning, I point to the pendant. "What an interesting piece of jewelry. Did your grandfather give it to you?"

Her eyes bug out and she sits forward. "He's here, isn't he?" Without waiting for an answer, she fumbles with the box and turns it on. It emits a broken part of song from a radio station, then turns to static. "Say something, *jiji!*"

"Jiji?" I question.

"Japanese for grandpa." She holds the box up and moves it around. "I'm listening," she tells him.

"What's going on out there?" Gloria calls.

"Nothing," Rosie and I say in unison.

Jiji says something in Japanese to Ophelia. All that comes through the radio is more static.

He looks at me and switches to English. I pass on his first message. "He says he's proud of you and your engineering skills."

"He is?" The girl glows, her body bobbing up and down on the chair. Her joy makes me smile. She touches the glass vial. "I have some of his ashes in this. I wear it close to my heart."

Rosie turns her belly sideways to my desk and speaks out the corner of her mouth. "I thought we had a no uninvited ghost policy right now."

Ghost whispering is much like ghost hunting, I suspect. It's a hit or miss game. "You win some, you lose some."

She turns back to Lia. "Before you leave, make sure I have that paperwork so we can pay you."

"If you're taking the *bookkeeping* job," I reiterate. "That's what I'm hiring you for." Not ghost hunting. That's the last thing I need—more spirits.

"You mean, I get paid?"

"I can only afford minimum wage, but yes, I plan to pay you."

"Oh, I'm taking it." She jumps up, sets the ghost box on my desk, and grabs a pen from my cup to fill out the form. "Ghosts and money? Best. Job. Ever!"

THIRTEEN

By five, I've officially hired Lia, finished up the fittings, and driven Gloria home. She's exhausted and I take a few minutes to get her into bed with a bowl of soup and a glass of tea before I leave. "Do you want me to come back later and check on you?"

"Don't be ridiculous." She brandishes her spoon in a dismissive gesture, pointing it at me. "I'm tired, not dead."

Thank goodness for that. "I'll call later instead. Deal?"

"You and your deals." She sips the drink and sighs, and I see past her impatient demeanor. Having someone take care of her, even if it's only temporary, isn't so bad. "I'm fine. Really. If you call and I sleep through it, which I most likely will, you'll be worried and drive over here. That will result in waking me up and neither of us will be happy. Go on, now. Stop fussing."

Her smile is genuine but doesn't quite reach her tired eyes. "I'll worry either way, and I refuse to feel guilty about doing so, but I'll go so you can rest." I tuck the comforter around her feet. "Promise you'll call if you need anything."

She half-heartedly rolls her eyes. "*Oui, oui.* Now leave this old lady alone to enjoy her soup, *cá va?*"

I squeeze her hand and let myself out. Ten minutes late to Hannah's, I find Sage has beaten me there and is in the kitchen chatting with the woman. The day's heat doesn't reach the interior, where it feels like an ice chest. I take over discussing things with Hannah and Sage excuses herself to install the cameras.

"Burt thinks I'm crazy." Hannah worries an embroidered hanky. "He hasn't said it, but I see it in his eyes. It's the same look Sharon gives me. Am I, Ava? Crazy, I mean?"

I sit in the seat Sage vacated. "Of course not. Ghosts *are* real, whether folks believe in them or not. But don't worry—we're going to stop Sly from haunting you, I promise."

There are two pill bottles on the table, and when her phone dings, she reaches for the fatter of the two. After shutting off the reminder, she shakes out a blue tablet and downs it with a gulp of tea. "He's going to break up with me, I just know it."

"A man whose been in love with you all these years, and finally has a chance to marry you? I bet you couldn't beat him off with a shovel. The look in his eyes is concern, nothing else."

Her surprise is evident. She stares at me for a long moment, then looks down, face flushing. "I don't know what you're talking about. We only fell in love a few months ago."

"You don't have to pretend. I know about the two of you."

The pink in her cheeks deepens and she stutters in frustration. "Wha... what? Oh my word. Are you psychic? You are, aren't you?" She frets and rocks back and forth, crying into the hanky. "Just like your aunt!"

Hardly. "Sharon favors him."

A nearly inaudible sob comes from her lips and she presses the material to them. Her voice drops to a whisper. "Oh, Lord. It was one time. One! I was lonely and grieving over my parents. I didn't know what to do. I just wanted to be loved, you know? Sly came home a few days later, and he looked so good in that uniform, and… I discovered I was pregnant shortly thereafter. Burt was already engaged and Sly wanted me back. Seemed like an easy fix."

"Ghosts seek revenge for such things. It's possible Sly is doing this because of the lie." If he has actually returned from the grave. I've still not seen nor heard him.

"Well, I can't undo it, and even if I could, I wouldn't. She's my daughter and I love her fiercely. She's the best thing, along with Burt, that's ever happened to me."

"Does she know?" I can't believe she hasn't figured it out. "Does he?"

"I've never told a soul." Her hand darts out and grabs mine. "Promise you won't, either."

I make a motion across my chest. "Cross my heart."

She stands and goes to the fridge, taking out a pitcher of tea. Her glass is half empty and she refills it. "Would you care for some?"

"No thanks. I'm going to finish drawing sigils on your house's foundations to keep unwanted ghosts out. I was interrupted the other night. Is that okay?"

"I guess."

Outside, I take a breath and locate the marker inside my bag. The humidity must be nearly as high as the summer temperature and my lungs struggle to inflate. I resume my job on the corner stones and keep an eye out for Sylvester and the young girl from the other day. Neither appears and I return to the kitchen a few minutes later, sweating and grateful for the air conditioning.

Sage is already inside, finishing her tea. Her bangs are matted to her forehead and she looks as hot as I am. "All done," she tells me. "Four cameras outside, a few others in here covering the main rooms, along with the hall." She grabs

Hannah's cell and opens an app, explaining the system to her. "The feeds are going to your phone, as well as to Ava's. The interior cameras can be disabled with this toggle for privacy." She demonstrates it to Hannah. "But I suggest leaving them active as much as you're comfortable with since the spirit has been hanging around inside."

Hannah nods. "You think we'll catch him?"

Sage hands her the phone. "If he materializes inside the house, or within a hundred yards in any direction, you bet we will."

"I'll have proof." Hannah squeezes her phone tight. "Then they'll know I'm not crazy."

Sage and I let ourselves out. "Thank you," I tell her. "I appreciate it."

"Our mom used to bring us here for peaches. We'd get peanuts, too, for our Cokes." Her gaze rakes over the landscape. "I liked Hannah back then, and I still do. If this ghost is bullying her, I want you to put a stop to it, Ava."

"I plan to."

That evening, I go through dozens of video clips, both from my place and Hannah's. No ghosts appear, although I have a lot of living folks going in and out of my house. I probably should shut the cameras off during business hours.

Logan brings me a glass of wine and massages my shoulders. He's changed out of his work clothes and into board shorts and polo shirt. "Dinner?"

"Yes, please. What sounds good?"

"I can grill chicken. I've got that seasoning mix with rosemary from Queenie I want to try."

He's in love with the new gas grill he bought a few weeks ago. I can't complain—I've been eating well and it saves time and prep in the evenings. "We've got fresh asparagus. I'll marinate it in olive oil and we can grill that, too."

"Throw in mashed potatoes and I'll love you forever."

"Anything for a man who feeds me." I grin and salute him with the glass. "Who knew you were so easy?"

We share a laugh and he heads off to crank up the grill. In the kitchen, I kick off my heels, wrap one of Aunt Willa's aprons around me and hum as I clean and oil the asparagus. All three cats and Moxley gather, hovering around my feet and nearly tripping me more than once. "You all have terrible manners. Shoo." I wave a hand at them. "It's not dinner time for you yet."

They move as far as the threshold between kitchen and living room. Logan comes in to retrieve the chicken and a pair of tongs. The sky has darkened and the air feels charged. I turn on a favorite playlist and put the sectioned potatoes on to boil. I've already microwaved them to get them started and they should be ready for mashing in no time.

Sherlock pops in while I'm searching for a stick of butter in the fridge. I really need to get to the grocery store before the end of the week. "It's behind the jam," he tells me.

I startle and hit my elbow on the door, sending it flying on its hinges to crash against the counter. "Ouch. What are you doing here?"

"At the moment, assisting you with locating the butter. I'm quite efficient at finding lost things."

He's correct about the hidden half stick and I snag it and bring it to the bowl. "You *are* wanted, by the way. Don't ever think you're not. I love having you around, and I know Paris, London, and Iula do, too." Those women work at the magical library, and although Sherlock is often condescending and moody, Paris has mentioned more than once that they miss him when he's hanging out with me.

His tone suggests he's insulted, wounded. "For finding trivial things like sticks of butter?"

"Sherlock, you've been invaluable in helping me solve several mysteries and you know it."

He raises his chin a notch, somewhat appeased. "Yet, your guardian angel has no use for me, and neither do your friends."

I want to finish cooking and enjoy my meal, but ghost drama comes first since this one is a friend as well. "I'm sorry about all of them being contrary to you, but I need you. Only... not right now. It's dinner time and I want to have a peaceful one with Logan. We have the wedding to discuss and I have a lot on my mind with Sly and Trysta."

"She knows," Sherlock announces.

Persephone appears near my side and I jump again. "You're not allowed to tell her that!"

His chin raises again, this time in defiance. "I can state the facts however, and to whomever, I wish."

"Who knows what?" I ask.

Persephone floats toward him. "Sherlock, do not—"

He hovers at the doorway near the cats. "Mrs. Cross."

Persephone makes a sound in her throat that suggests she's going to kill him. *If* that were possible, I have no doubt she would. "That's none of your business, you meddling spirit!"

"Stop," I tell her. My stomach falls. "How did she find out?" I ask Sherlock.

"Trysta told her."

Persephone shakes her head and moves to the table. "You've overstepped. Again. This won't go well for you, you know."

Logan rushes in. "The sky looks stormy. We better get the asparagus cooking."

I take a breath, slide the veggie pieces into a grill basket, and smile at him as if it's just us and the animals. "Here you go."

He heads out and I turn to the ghost. "How did Trysta find out?"

"She didn't," Persephone insists, "and Helen doesn't have a clue. He's making it up."

I don't believe her, but I'm more worried about Sherlock at the moment.

"Let them come," he counters the angel's previous statement. "Let them take me. I don't care anymore. If I can't..." He glances between me and her, and I see he's miserable. "Any dimension is better than here."

"Whoa, whoa, whoa." I hold up a hand. "You mean you want to cross to the afterlife?"

"Yes. Fine. Make the doorway." He motions at me. The cats near his feet watch the show with interest, all eyes on me as if they understand. "Make sure I'm deposited as far from her"—he points at the angel—"as possible."

She's broken his heart, and with the rejection from Brax and Rhys, he's being rash. "This decision shouldn't be made in the heat of an argument." I wipe my hands on the apron and glance around for the wine bottle. "Let's all take a breath and talk this out."

Which is the last thing I want to do, but he's hurting and I can't ignore it.

"There's nothing to discuss." Persephone draws out a chair and sits. "There are rules and he's violated them more than once."

I've never heard about any such thing when it comes to the spirit world. "What kind of rules? Is there, like, a handbook or something?" Sure would be handy.

"She's told me things." Sherlock stares defiantly past both of us, nose in the air. "Things I was not supposed to pass on to you. What good is a guardian angel if she doesn't help you?"

I've asked myself that more than once. "Now I understand." This is the guardian angel rule about helping me with ghost problems but not giving me the answers. Shoot, I almost believed there was, indeed, a guide for the spirit world. Maybe I need to write my own. "It sounds as if Persephone violated the rules, not you." I return to the potatoes, now boiling hard, and lower the gas. "Sherlock, I'm not crossing you until you calm down and make your decision based on reason and not emotions." I actually hope he decides to stay. I like him and he's been more helpful than Persephone with my ghost whispering. "We need to talk about this in more depth, but perhaps now isn't the time."

Sam appears and sniffs the air. "Food!" He bends down to stare Tabitha in her golden eyes. "Please do magic on me. I want to be human again so I can eat. I want to read books. I shall do whatever you want, my dear. Just bring me back for a few minutes so I can experience life again!"

"No," both Persephone and I say in unison.

"No magic and no bringing the dead back to life," I continue. Tabby purrs and rubs against his leg. The energy in the room goes electric and thunder booms outside. My grandmother has been known to do whatever she wants and she seems to enjoy defying me. I see a light in her eyes and I swear she grins. "Tabby..." I warn.

She morphs into her human self. Naked, like always. Sam holds out his arms and she falls into them, kissing him passionately.

Apparently food and books aren't the only things he'd like to re-experience.

Sherlock and Persephone begin bickering. Sam pleads with Tabitha again. Arthur and Lancelot hide under the table, whether from the thunder or the spirits, who knows. Moxley howls.

"Enough!" I shout over the din. "All of you! I'm going to eat a quiet and enjoyable meal with my fiancé. No crossing ghosts and no magic to bring Sam back to life, not even for a few minutes. Get some clothes on and go do…whatever…at the homestead. I will deal with each of you later. For now, OUT."

Logan enters, the platter of chicken in one hand and the basket of asparagus in the other. Hearing my outburst, he pulls up short. Another peal of thunder echoes over the house. "Everything okay?" he asks.

"Sure," I say, ignoring the ghosts, angel, and shapeshifting cat. The food smells amazing and I inhale deeply. The scent of rain trails after him. "Everything is peachy."

I reach for the food, stomach rumbling nearly as loudly as the thunder. Before I can accept it, however, a crack of lightning splits the night beyond the window and the lights flicker once and go out.

FOURTEEN

P lunged into sudden darkness, the platter and basket crash to the floor.

"Are you okay?" Logan asks.

"No," I reply, feeling a warm, furry body rush past my legs, going for the grilled meat. "I'm hungry and tired, and I just want to enjoy our dinner!"

I sound slightly hysterical. Logan moves close and my eyes adjust to the shadows as he rubs my arms and draws me to his chest. "There are still two pieces on the grill. I'll get those and you grab your flashlight, okay?"

I do as he says, chasing the cats away from the ruined meal on the floor and locating my light in the junk drawer, along with a few candles. Pieces of asparagus are everywhere. I toss the wasted food into the trash as Logan returns, soaked from the now pouring rain. "They're a bit wet," he says, setting them on a clean plate, "but better than nothing."

By candlelight, I call Gloria and get her landline's answering machine. Before I can stew, she calls me back, telling me she's fine and not to worry. I add butter and milk to the soft potatoes and mash out my frustration, while Logan changes into dry clothes. When he returns, he pours glasses of sweet tea to round out our make-shift meal and we descend on the food like it's ambrosia.

The candles add a nuance to the dinner and Logan does his best to lighten the mood, telling me about a scene with a woman dressed in a bunny costume at the courthouse earlier that day. She was protesting an ordinance concerning how many pets a person could own inside the town boundaries and had garnered quite a bit of publicity with the stunt. The lengths some people will go to make a point never ceases to amaze me. Of course, between the two of us, we're pushing the limit, so I applaud her stand on the subject.

The storm continues to rage outside. The pets have deserted us, in search of hiding places, and the ghosts are nowhere to be seen. Fine with me. I desperately want to tell Logan what I've discovered about Hannah and her family, but I've sworn not to expose her secret. It feels wrong keeping it from him, but I have to for now.

"Sherlock claims your mother knows about our plan for the secret wedding," I tell him. "Persephone says she doesn't."

He toys with the final bite on his plate. "Who do you believe?"

I'm not sure it matters, but... "Sherlock."

He sits back and stretches. "If Mother knew, she would have already eviscerated me."

True. Maybe I'm predisposed to believe the worst about my guardian angel. "Sherlock claims Trysta told her."

"Trysta?" He scowls. "How would she know?"

"She *is* a ghost." At least, we think she is. "You know what Winter says about the dead knowing everything."

"That's a scary thought."

"Isn't it, though? Anyway, just a warning in case Helen has been informed. We might need to prepare a counterstrike."

Across the table, he smiles and light dances over his face, giving him a mischievous look. "I like how you think. What say you, general? Should we feign innocence or strike first and admit we were considering it, but changed our minds?"

My phone goes off in the other room. "That's Daddy. We should weigh our options in greater depth after I answer that."

I'm halfway to my office and the ringing phone when the front door opens. Two people burst in, a shared umbrella between them and blocking my view of their faces. "Hi, neighbor," Charles booms as water runs off his trench coat onto the floor. "What a night, huh?"

I stop in my tracks. "What a night," I echo as Trysta emerges as well.

"I surely hate storms, what with the lightning and all." She looks as dry as I am, grinning at me as she proffers a tray. "We brought cupcakes!"

"Of course you did." The phone rings again, then cuts off as the call goes to voicemail. The EMF device beeps like mad when she steps closer.

Her head turns in its direction. "What's that awful noise?"

I glance around to make sure there are no other ghosts in the space with us, then face her. "A detector for spirit activity."

"A what?" Charles asks. "Oh, jeez. You're not peddling that mediumship baloney again, are you?"

Trysta leans toward the room with a frown. Illumination from the streetlight casts a glow across the furniture. "Looks like it's coming from that bear on the shelf. Is the thing haunted?"

I grit my teeth. "How is it you're in my house?"

Charles wipes his feet on the rug and lowers the umbrella.

"That's not very neighborly of you, Ava. You're acting strange tonight."

"Is it the storm, honey?" Trysta asks. "They give me the creeps, too."

Logan enters and greetings are exchanged. Charles ditches the umbrella and removes a bottle of dark liquid from inside his trench. He looks more pale and drawn under his smile. "Best brandy around, my brother. Get the glasses."

Logan pats my back in a show of support. "Ava and I were just..." he begins, but can't seem to come up with a lie that sounds plausible.

I help him out. "Going to bed early. Sorry. We're both exhausted."

"Oh, but with this storm, you won't be able to sleep anyway." Trysta brushes past me heading for the kitchen. On her way, she gives Logan a slow perusal.

An explicative slips from my lips and Charles frowns as she enters the kitchen. "She really does hate storms. Something to do with an accident when she was a kid. Bad day, Ava?"

"Yes." I peer through the gloom after Trysta. "And it just got—"

Logan pinches my side before I can say "worse."

Regrouping, I face his brother again. "What kind of accident?"

He shrugs. "Something to do with her dad. He used to take her to the beach during storms because he thought it was cool. Scared the starch right out of her."

Logan shoots me a glance. Must be the lightning strike that put Larry into a coma. "Has she told you much about her family?" I ask Charles.

He lowers his voice, glancing toward the other room. "Her parents died when she was young, and she ended up in foster care. Had a rough time, and she doesn't care to talk about it."

I bet she doesn't. "That's too bad," I say.

"Well, we're glad you're here," Logan tells his brother.

I gape at him. "We are?"

"Yes, we are." He chuckles and pulls me closer. "Ava and I want to talk to you two about the upcoming wedding. She has ideas for the ceremony she wants to share with Trysta, don't you, sweetheart? And you and I need to discuss the bachelor party," he says to Charles.

His brother raises the bottle in salute. "You bet we do."

As he trails after Trysta, Logan draws me into my office and tells me in a hushed tone, "Nothing is keeping her out, so we need a new plan. Instead of pushing her away, you need to earn her confidence. Get her to open up, find the chink in her ghostly armor."

I see where he's going. "Keep our enemies close and all that."

"Exactly. What do you think?"

It's an option, although I'm not excited about it. "I'll give it a try, but if I kill her, and she's not actually a ghost, will you help me bury the body?"

He looks affronted. "Do you even have to ask?"

We exchange wicked grins. My phone beeps, letting me know Daddy's left a message. "One hour, no more. I'll be as friendly as I can, but I make no promises. I can't indulge her longer than that."

He nods and kisses me. "You're a good woman, Ava Fantome."

"Make sure Chuck pours me some of that brandy, and don't eat the cupcakes."

"Charles looks ill, don't you think?"

Yes, I do. "She's draining his energy faster than I expected."

"Man, I hate this. There's got to be something we can do."

I squeeze his arm. "I'll join you after I get Daddy's voicemail."

After another quick kiss on the cheek, he leaves.

"What a storm, huh?" Daddy asks, when I call him back. "Lightning blew a transformer. You kids okay?"

I wish I could blow Trysta's transformer. "Fine, Daddy."

"The reason I called, besides checking on you, of course, is to let you know about Hannah's husband."

"Did you find something?"

"Nothing yet, but I thought you might want to know Sly owed thousands of dollars to a bookie named Boom Boom Mathers. He had a huge gambling debt and a price on his head, and there was speculation at the time, at least by me, that Sly faked his death. We had no proof, however, and it was, as you know, ruled death by animal mauling. I was thinking it over, though, and I did a search on Boom Boom. Found his obit. He died two weeks ago."

"And?"

"Could be Sly is coming out of hiding."

This gives me pause. "His debt disappeared with Boom Boom's death?"

"Possibly. I'm sure Boom Boom has a successor but it's probably a competitor. Sly's debt from twenty years ago was more than likely wiped off the books after he was declared deceased. With the bookie dead, too, he's in the clear."

"Why go after Hannah, though? If he's alive and living under a false identity, why come back here?"

"Gambling is an addiction. It's doubtful he suddenly went cold turkey after faking his death."

"And he needs money."

Daddy makes a *ding-ding-ding* noise. "He could claim amnesia and they were never technically divorced, according to what she told you, so... Even if she decides to follow through now, there was no prenup, so legally he may be entitled to half her assets. I'm no attorney, but I bet he could make a case for himself."

The idea angers me. I remember her saying she saw a reflection in the window at the library. "Do you believe he's still alive? That he could be that clever and cunning?"

"I think it's a strong possibility, and if something happens to Hannah, and she hasn't changed her will, he could inherit everything she has left."

"That's a strong reason to stop her from marrying Burt or kill her off."

"He's at least setting her up to make folks think she's nuttier than a fruitcake, and when she turns up dead, it will look like an accident."

My stomach revolts. "I've got security cameras set up at her house. What else can we do, in case your theory is right?"

"Good thinking on those. I'll talk to Landon in the morning, see if he can keep an eye on her, but until I find evidence that supports my speculation, there's nothing much we can do."

FIFTEEN

Five minutes in to winning Trysta's confidence, I want to stab my eyes out with a fork.

She babbles on and on about her business, her love of baking, and the upcoming nuptials. At one point, she insists on viewing my gowns to see if she likes any of them.

At least this gives me something *I* enjoy talking about. She insists on trying on the Belle and the Winter.

In the small changing room down the hall, I give her as much privacy as possible, but both dresses are voluminous and she requires help to get into them. Neither are her size, so I use clips to hold the straining fabric together in the back and allow her to play dress-up with a veil and accessories. The whole time, I keep trying to see the male spirits attached to her, but they don't become visible, no matter how much I reach out to them.

What I do spot, in the low candlelight, is a whitish scar on her left thigh. It's jagged, approximately eight inches in length, and the skin is puckered. When she catches me assessing it, she covers it quickly with the layers of the gown. If she were a normal bridal client, I would apologize for my poor manners, but she's not, so I don't.

Once she's squeezed into the Belle, I walk her out to the showroom area, which is a renovated end of the living room.

"Chucky!" she calls, twirling around on the slightly raised dais. Even with a couple of candles, she has to squint to see herself in the floor to ceiling mirror. "What do you think of this one?"

Charles and Logan bring their drinks and join us. Charles is carrying the tray of cupcakes, a few less on it than previously. "You look stunning," he says, wide-eyed. "But then, you're the most beautiful woman in the world. You could wear a gunny sack and I'd still be nuts for you. Isn't it bad luck to see you in the dress before the big moment?"

"Aww, you're so sweet." She does a little dip and glances at me. "Isn't he the best?"

"The best," I echo. I only hope he lives to make it to the wedding—if we can't prevent it. Logan hands me his glass, and I knock back the liquor in one gulp. It's excellent brandy, that's for sure, but it still burns on the way down.

"What do you think, Logi?" She smiles demurely at him.

I try not to vomit.

Logan freezes, a deer caught in headlights. "It's a very pretty dress."

Nice save. I lean into him, grateful he's such a good guy, and he relieves me of the glass.

"Your figure would be better showcased in my Bellamy," I tell her.

"Now that *is* a great gown." Logan nods enthusiastically. "You should try that one on, too."

Lifting the skirt, she pokes out a naked foot to step off the dais and holds out a hand for him to steady her. "You never said if you liked my cinnamon cupcakes."

"Oh, man," Charles says, "aren't those the bomb? I love those things." He pats his growing midsection, and snags a cake from the tray. He's sweating profusely. "Too bad they don't love me!"

We all chuckle along, but I see Trysta staring at Logan. "I love to keep my men happy," she says.

Men. Plural. "Let's get you out of this." I grab her arm and steer her to the dressing room.

She trips, falling into Logan. He rights her and she strokes his arm. "Thanks, honey."

Charles remains oblivious. Or maybe he's drunk. Hard to tell as he finishes off the cupcake in two bites and lifts his empty glass in the air. "Time for a refill."

Trysta takes a cupcake as we pass the tray. In the changing room, I unclip the back of the dress and assist her in stepping out of it. Thunder rocks the house and lightning flashes on its heels.

She half-trips again, for real this time, and nearly slams the treat into my face. Shaking, she sets it on the side table. "I don't know what's come over me." She fans her face. "I'm feeling so...odd."

Could it be that the ghost-proofing *is* having an effect? Maybe it's keeping out her battery chargers. I point to a chair. "You better sit down. Would you like some water?"

She shakes her head and drops into the seat in only her slip and underwear. The scar is on display, but I ignore it. She raises her hands to her head and blinks several times. "I usually feel so light and happy when I'm here, but tonight, it feels ...different."

"Different, how?"

"Must be the storm, that's all."

Candlelight creates shadows, but draws my eyes to something gleaming on her upper chest. A necklace with three thin gold chains, connected at the back, and hanging in graduating lengths. Tiny charms dangle from each one. I hadn't noticed it earlier, but they appear to be rectangular lockets, each with a clasp.

My mind flashes to Lia and her grandfather's ashes. "What a pretty necklace. It looks vintage." I touch one of the filigreed pieces. "Are there pictures inside?"

"It was my...grandmother's." She fingers the lowest of the three lockets, lying near her heart, and brushes my hand away in the process. "No pictures, I just liked it. One of the only things I have of hers."

I'd bet my whole collection of gowns that Mama Nightengale is right and those lockets contain pieces of 'organic' matter from the men she's been using to keep her physical body charged. "Did she pass?"

"A long time ago."

"And your father?"

Her lips purse and she closes her eyes, swaying slightly. "He's dead, too."

Thinking of Larry and his coma, I remember the man in the hospital elevator. He mentioned his wife was in one, yet I could see and hear her spirit. The thought gives me pause, and an idea tickles the back of my brain. "Charles said you hate storms due to an accident when you were a kid." I point to the scar. "Is that how you ended up with that?"

One hand slides her slip lower to cover the old injury. "It was a long time ago. Wrong place, wrong time, is all."

Was she hit by the bolt that put her father in a coma? "When it happened, was there some kind of energy exchange between you and Larry?"

Her face shows a combination of fear and surprise at the name, then she wipes it blank. "I don't know what you're talking about."

She sways again, and I reach to steady her. If I yank the necklace off, like removing a plug from a socket, will the connection between her and her ghostly battery packs be broken?

Can't hurt to try.

The yellow light dances across her features and her bottom lip quivers. Then I realize it's not only her lip—her chin is trembling, her body seeming almost translucent. The ends of her hair lift and she realizes it and bats it down. "Storms do this to me," she says by way of explanation. "Since the accident, I have odd reactions to the electricity they generate."

I blink to clear my vision, but feel a spurt of near giddiness that I may have the answer to getting rid of her. I ignore the fact that her shoulder, which I'm holding on to, feels extremely solid under my fingers. "I know what you are, Stacey," I say above the noise overhead. "It's time for you to cross. You're not meant to be on this plane anymore and what you've done to those men in order to keep yourself here in the physical world isn't right."

Her eyes go wide and she places a hand over all three lockets. "Stacey? Are you drunk?"

In one swift motion, I tear her hand away and give the necklace a jerk. The hook at the back breaks and the layers of chains cascade down her collarbone and into my hand. "No more stealing other people's energy. You're done."

She comes to her feet, her body shuddering as though she's having spasms. "What is wrong with you? You've been acting so rude tonight."

That's when I see the unanchored tethers, silver in the dark room, blinking in and out. Three of them lead to the front door. Another snakes out toward the kitchen. It's thinner and more transparent, but I know it's the reason Charles looks so ghastly.

Closing my eyes, I focus on making the lighted heavenly doorway. "Go to the light," I tell all of them.

Next thing I know, Trysta shoves me. For a ghost with no electrical cords anymore, she's incredibly strong. I lose my balance and my foot catches on the table leg. I fall to a knee, dropping the necklace when I throw my hand out to stop my nosedive.

She snatches it up, then takes her cupcake and smashes it into my face. "How dare you! I don't know what game you're playing, Ava, but you're acting crazy as a loon. You've broken my favorite necklace!"

As I hastily wipe frosting from my eyes and wobble to my feet, she shoves me again, pushing me out of her way. Gathering her clothes, she doesn't even take time to put them on, stomping past me in her slip.

The sugary cake fills one nostril and sticks to my upper lip. Frantically, I use the back of my hand to rub off what's on my mouth.

Why didn't she turn spectral? I can't see the ghosts previously hooked to her now, either. Did they cross, or is she connected to them again? "Wait," I call. I can't let her leave with that jewelry. I step on fallen chunks of cupcake, and realize I've blown this big time. I've got to get her to stay and cross to the afterlife. I need another way to reason with her. "Trysta, I'm...sorry." I choke on the word.

She marches to the front door, Charles and Logan emerging from the kitchen once more. "Baby?" Charles looks dumbfounded. "Where are you going?"

"Home," she sobs, whirling once she reaches the exit to glare at me. "I know where I'm not wanted." She turns the knob, but throws another parting snarl my way. "And I wouldn't be caught dead in one of your ugly gowns!"

Charles and Logan turn their heads in unison to regard me, then Charles runs after her, not bothering to snatch up the umbrella, trench coat, or close the door behind him as they race into the pouring rain.

Humid air sweeps into the house. The gargoyles outside yell curses at the fleeing couple, which they can't hear. Could be a trick of light, but I swear I see the three ghosts hovering after them, connected to Trysta once more.

Logan grabs a dishtowel and hands it to me. "That went well."

Shoulder-to-shoulder, we watch them run across the street and enter the bakery. I use the towel to clean my face. "I handled that all wrong."

He places an arm around my shoulders. "You'll get her next time. One positive? There's no body to bury in this storm."

I snort. "She now knows that I'm aware she's a ghost. If there *is* a next time, it won't go any easier, I guarantee."

"When have you ever done anything the easy way?"

"Touché."

My phone rings. I don't feel like answering it, but it could be Gloria. Logan shuts the door and locks it. "Want me to get it?"

"Nah, I'll do it. Can you clean up the crumbs in the changing room? I don't want our pets to eat them."

Sam pops in, appearing right in my face and scaring me half to death. "Jeez," I say, my hand going to my chest. "Don't do that."

"I am truly sorry," he says, "but Miss Hannah is in dire circumstances."

My blood runs cold and I race to the phone in my office. "Hannah," I answer, knowing it's her. "Everything okay?"

She sobs and the hair on my neck stands up like it's electrified. "Oh, Ava, I'm so scared. Something *terrible* has happened and I don't know what to do."

"What is it?"

"Sly got to Burt." Her voice shakes and comes out so quietly, I have trouble understanding her. "He's here, and I'm next!"

Frigid air races down my spine. "What do you mean he got to Burt?"

Another high pitched sob. "He's unconscious on the bedroom floor. There's blood...*everywhere.*"

I race for my coat, snatching it off the hook. "Call 911. I'll be there in ten minutes."

A jittery laugh bubbles up from her throat. "You'll be too late. All of you. Sly's going to kill me."

"Hannah, stay on the line." Logan has heard my voice and comes quickly to check on me. I move the phone from my mouth and tell him Burt is injured and I have to go to Hannah. He helps me with my coat and grabs his.

"I can't," she says in a resigned voice. "Goodbye, Ava."

The line goes dead.

SIXTEEN

The ride to the farm is harrowing with the storm. Logan is a good driver, but he has to reduce speed several times where the roads are flooded.

By the time we arrive, an ambulance and two squad cars are already present. At least she took my advice and called for help. While one of the cops tries to bar us from going inside, Logan claims to be Hannah's attorney and states he has the right to speak to her immediately.

The good thing is, the electricity is on. Her house is lit up like a landing strip. We shed our dripping coats, jumping out of the way as Reverend Stout, who moonlights as a first responder, wheels Burt on a gurney past us, along with another EMT. Blood seeps through the bandages wrapped around his head and his skin has a gray cast to it. He is unconscious.

I ask where Hannah is. Stout juts his chin toward the rear of the house as the two of them ease the front wheels over the threshold. "She's hysterical. I offered her a sedative, but she refused. Keeps talking about her dead husband getting his revenge. I think she needs *your* kind of help, Ava."

The good vicar and I had an experience last month with a spirit who'd possessed him. He's not keen on what I do, but he now acknowledges and accepts my ghost whispering in a more open manner. "I'll talk to her. Will Burt be okay?"

He glances toward the top of the stairs. I hear the familiar voice of Detective Jones and someone else talking, probably in the bedroom. In a lowered voice, he tells me, "Looks like someone hit him in the head more than once with Hannah's own shotgun. Better than shooting him, I guess, but head injuries are unpredictable, and he's sustained several blows."

"What are you doing here?"

The booming voice echoes around the stairwell and we all glance up to find Jones glaring down on us. Stout and the other paramedic hustle Burt out and Logan places a hand on my lower back. "Hannah called us," he tells the gruff detective whose size is twice as menacing on his lofty perch.

He begins his descent down the wooden stairs, his weight making them creak and groan. "Why would Mrs. Grady want either of you here?"

Logan steers me toward the kitchen. "We're about to find out."

At first, I don't see her when we enter. She's huddled in a in the corner of the room against the lower cabinets. No longer crying, her eyes are still bloodshot and remote, as though she's a million miles away.

"Hannah?" I bend down beside her. "It's Ava. Are you okay?"

Her stare is blank. "I'm so sorry."

"I haven't finished interrogating her," Jones says. "You need to wait in the living room."

I don't bother arguing and stay focused on Hannah. "Sorry for what?"

"Ava." Jones warns.

Hannah grips my arm. "He's here. He's trying to kill me."

"Not this again." Jones mumbles.

Her wild eyes search my face. "You said he wanted revenge. He's going to get it, too. First Burt, then Sharon. He wants me to suffer. But he's going to kill me in the end."

She bursts out crying and Logan hands her his hand-kerchief.

Jones does a poor job of keeping the frustration out of his voice. "Sylvester is long dead, Mrs. Grady. He can't hurt you."

I'm torn. I haven't seen, heard, or sensed the man's spirit. I also have zero proof he's *not* haunting her. "It doesn't matter," I tell the detective. "If Hannah believes he can hurt her, he can."

"Riiiight." Jones sighs so audibly I feel it in my bones. "She's talking nonsense and you are, too. Reverend Stout couldn't find anything physically wrong with her, but maybe she has other issues. You know what I mean?"

When I glance up, he's making a whirling motion around his temple with one finger, then directs it at the bottles of medication on the table. I half-wonder again if Hannah *is* seeing things that aren't there, but since I can't rule out that whatever is happening isn't ghost-induced, I feel responsible. "We'll take care of her."

"Is that frosting in your hair?" Jones asks.

I touch my locks, and sure enough, my fingers come away with sticky stuff. "Don't ask."

He stares at the woman on the floor, then says to us, "I'm afraid I have to hold her for further questioning."

"Why?" Logan asks.

"There's no evidence that anyone was in the house except her and Mr. Dietmar."

I come to my feet, the suggestion in his tone not sitting well with me. "What are you saying?"

"The weapon our victim was struck with repeatedly belongs to her."

She's a suspect? I don't ask it out loud, but I see Jones is considering his next step. "You can't believe Hannah would do this."

"Unless you can find proof that someone else was here, I have no other option."

The cameras. I pull out my phone and bring up the video clips. "I just might be able to do that."

Jones and Logan peer over my shoulders as I scan the short videos. Exterior snippets catch Burt arriving at six-thirty with flowers and a bottle of wine. Interior shots catch the two in an embrace, Hannah going on about the flowers, and then heading down the hallway to the kitchen with Burt trailing behind.

"Why do you have these?" Jones asks. "Do I need to arrest you, as well?"

"Hannah asked me to set up security cameras and keep an eye on her place." I flip to the next outside shot right before the storm. A rabbit darts across the backyard, as if scared from its hole. I squint, rewind the segment and watch again. "What is that?"

Logan takes my phone and zooms in on the shadow I've pointed to. "Could be a man."

Jones leans in. "Or a shadow from a tree."

"It's a person." I'm sure of it. "See the way the shadows are darker here?" I outline the figure. "Looks like he's wearing a hood."

Jones scowls. "You sure it's not a *ghost*?"

No, but I don't care for the sarcasm lacing his voice. I walk to the kitchen window and stare at the backyard lined to the east with a grove of peach trees. The clouds overhead cast everything in gloom. "Whoever it was startled the rabbit from its hiding spot, which was there." I direct their mutual gazes to the area. But how did our culprit enter the house without being caught on camera? There has to be one in the dozens of clips that shows it.

Jones shrugs. "Even if an attacker was hiding there, all traces of him are gone after that gully washer." When I start to protest, he holds up a hand. "I'll still have an officer check it out."

I take my phone, plunk down in a chair, and continue to scan the clips. "If he entered the place, we've got him on video."

"He was here," Hannah says, voice shaking. "He was waiting in the bedroom when we went in."

"You didn't mention that." Jones studies her. "What time was it?"

She thinks for a moment. "Seven-thirty, maybe? We ate dinner and watched Wheel of Fortune, but I was so tired, I could barely keep my eyes open. Burt insisted I take a pill and call it a night. He walked me upstairs to the bedroom, and then..." She visibly shivers. "Sly came out of nowhere. He hit Burt over and over again."

"Was he wearing a hood?" Logan asks.

She inclines her head once. "Yes, a hunting jacket, with a hood."

Jones scribbles that down. "Did you see the attacker's face?"

Her bottom lip quivers, making her jowls tremble. "No, but it was him. It was my ex-husband."

Jones' jaw firms, frustration once more evident.

"Why didn't Sly shoot Burt?" I ask, wondering if Burt got a look at his features. When he gains consciousness, can he tell us who it was? "Why beat him with the gun?"

"He tried to shoot." Hannah's head bobs erratically. "I'd taken the shells out after Sharon left. I never liked loaded guns in the house."

Something niggles at my brain, but is gone again when Jones asks, "If you didn't see his face, why are you so sure it was Sylvester?"

She doesn't hesitate. "The smell."

"Excuse me?"

Fingers trembling, she uses a handkerchief to wipe at her eyes before she curls into herself again. "He smelled like he always did when he came home from the lodge."

We all frown. "What lodge?" Jones asks.

Her weak gaze meets his. "The hunting lodge, out along the bluff. It belongs to Russ Goldstein."

Logan crosses his arms. "I know that place. The property line backs up to the vineyard. No one's used it in ten, fifteen years? It's a rundown disaster. Mother complains about it all the time, but the Goldsteins left town ages ago and it fell into disuse." He bends down and asks Hannah, "How exactly did the lodge smell?"

"Musty." Her eyes get that far away look. "They only used it in the fall, and it sat empty and closed up the rest of the year. I'd have a devil of a time getting the odor out of his clothes and jackets. And chicory. He used to drink chicory infused vodka. Claimed it was coffee, but I knew what it was. He and the others did more drinking than hunting."

"The man who attacked Burt tonight smelled like chicory and mustiness." Jones no longer sounds certain there wasn't an actual attacker, but he puts the notepad away. "You check the rest of those security tapes and let me know if you find anything more conclusive," he says to me. "I'll check the lodge first thing tomorrow."

I wish ghosts didn't have odors so I could cross the option of Sly's spirit off my list, and press for Daddy's hypothesis that the man is still alive. However, occasionally, I do pick up their aftershave or perfume or even a favorite flavor of chewing gum.

If they were a smoker in life, chances are, I'll catch a whiff of cigarette or pipe smoke when they're near. And while a ghost that has enough juice to beat a man with a gun seems highly improbable, poltergeists have been known to do serious harm to folks.

Either way—ghost or human—I can't leave Hannah alone, and I don't believe she's bananas, regardless of her current state of mind. I reach for her hand. "You're coming home with us."

Her eyes focus on me. "I am?"

"She is?" Logan echoes.

"Don't leave town, Mrs. Grady," Jones orders, heading for the doorway. "I may have more questions for you in the morning."

His heavy footsteps reverberate down the hall. "Has anyone called Sharon to let her know about Burt?" I call after him.

"She's been notified," he yells back.

"I'll get her into the car if you want to grab a few of her things," Logan tells me, taking Hannah's hand from mine.

Jones has superior hearing. "Stay out of the bedroom. It's a crime scene!"

I roll my eyes. "Whatever," I mutter.

THE RAIN HAS STOPPED COMPLETELY and the electricity is on at my place when we arrive home. The cats are lolling on various pieces of furniture and Moxley greets us at the door with a loud "woof."

Logan makes over him and I lead Hannah to the guest room. She said nothing on the ride, falling asleep and snoring before we hit the outskirts of town.

Her steps falter on the stairs and she grips the railing tightly. "I hate to be an imposition."

Persephone appears on the landing. "What happened to her? Did the ghost attack again?"

I nod at her and speak to Hannah. "It's no problem." The woman needs a guardian angel more than I do. "You've had a rough few days. You're safe here." I only hope that's true.

Inside the room, I place Hannah's overnight bag on the window seat before I retrieve fresh linens. She revives enough to help me sheet the bed and then we say goodnight.

Downstairs, I fix a cup of herbal tea and Logan rubs circles with his thumb on the back of my neck as it steeps. "What are we going to do about these ghosts?"

"No idea. Things are out of control and I'm feeling helpless to handle either of them."

"You're sure Trysta and Sly *are* ghosts, right?"

I face him and feel the weight of the world on my shoulders. "Honestly, I'm not, anymore." I tell him about Daddy's theory.

"Sylvester faked his death?"

"It's possible." Something is still niggling at my brain, and I think over everything that's happened in the past few days. "Sharon told me her mother would sit downstairs after he died with the loaded shotgun on her lap, fearing he would return in the middle of the night and harm them."

He leans against the counter. "What an awful way to live."

"Tonight, Hannah said she never liked having a loaded gun in the house."

"Conflicting stories." His attorney brain jumps on board. "You can ask her to clarify in the morning." He hands me my cup and guides me out of the kitchen. "You need rest."

My eyes close the moment my head hits the pillow, the tea undrunk. I wake sometime later when I hear the sound of heavy footsteps on the stairs.

SEVENTEEN

I sit straight up in bed, pulse hammering in my ears. My dreams were filled with menacing hunters and blood. Women's screams. One of them lingers in my brain, like a cobweb, and I run a hand over my face to try and clear it.

As my hearing normalizes, I listen closely, but catch nothing unusual in the old house. A few squeaks, the fridge running downstairs. I speculate I've dreamed the footsteps.

Or maybe Hannah got up to use the restroom or get a glass of water. I swing my feet over the edge of the bed and grab my robe.

Out in the hall, I see no lights on under her door or the bathroom. I start to call out but if Hannah is sleeping, I don't want to wake her.

A fissure of fear runs down my neck. Could her attacker have followed us home?

Back in my room, I grab the stun gun from my bag and slip my feet into my house shoes. Quietly, I make my way down the stairs, using the faint light from the single window to see by.

As I hit the landing, I hear the click of the front door. My heart nearly stops. Is it Trysta? Sly?

Readying the weapon, I pause when Logan steps out from his first floor room. "What's going on?" He yawns, then raises a brow when he notices what I'm carrying. "Is someone here?"

Tabby races past, making me shriek and I nearly drop the stun gun. "I'm not sure," I whisper. "I think someone was."

Logan takes it and pulls me behind him. He flips on the lights and together we step into the living room.

The mirror at the far end reflects our pajama-clad selves back to us. His hair is tousled in a sexy manner, while mine is sticking out at odd angles. We continue to the main room where my desk and Rosie's sit undisturbed.

No ghosts or humans jump out at us, and the EMF detector is quiet. Tabby is in the front display window and glances over her shoulder at me. She emits a high-pitched wail.

I break free from Logan's grip and run to the window. A car is driving off from out front.

Logan comes up behind me. "Who was that?"

"Sharon." Sam floats next to me. "She picked up her mother."

I repeat what he's said to Logan, and then ask, "Why? Are they going to see Burt?"

Sam shakes his head. Persephone appears. "They're going to see Sly," she says.

My stomach pitches. "Get your keys," I tell Logan. "We need to follow them."

IT DOESN'T TAKE LONG for us to catch up to the blue sedan. Logan keeps his headlights off and stays a safe distance behind. While he drives, I speculate on what Persephone said, the angel no longer around to question. "Why in the world would Sharon take Hannah to see Sly if he's still alive? He's attacked her and Burt! Sharon told me she hated him."

"You should call Detective Jones and let him know what's going on."

"Not until I have proof that Persephone is correct. They could be going to the grave where they buried an empty coffin in his honor. I don't need Jones being irate with me if we're wrong. I just can't believe Hannah would have anything to do with Sylvester if he's still alive. Could Sharon have lied to her to get her in the car?"

"Won't know until we see where they're going and what they're doing."

I realize he's attempting to focus on the dark road and not have an accident. I close my mouth and do the same. When they take the turn leading out of town instead of toward the clinic, I know they're not visiting the hospital or cemetery.

If they are meeting up with Sly, I'm going to be all kinds of angry.

I wish I'd changed my clothes, but there was no time. Once again, I mentally rehash the conversations I had with Hannah and Sharon. Sharon seemed quite familiar with the shotgun, where I never saw Hannah touch the thing. Yet, Sharon stated she hated her father and what he did to their family, so what motive would she have to cause her mother's injuries or harm Burt in the name of Sly?

We find ourselves passing the vineyard, a lone light illuminating the drive. Logan says, "I know where they're going."

I realize it at the same time. "The old lodge."

The path narrows as the road rises in elevation and eventually becomes gravel. The trees lining the way thicken and potholes have us bouncing so hard, I nearly knock enamel from my clashing teeth. I text Daddy, telling him my suspicions. He doesn't respond, probably because he's asleep.

I consider calling Jones, but I still have nothing but a woman and her daughter driving out to an abandoned building in the middle of the night. It's not a crime, and I can't exactly tell him my guardian angel claims they're meeting a supposed dead man.

By the time we arrive, Logan has slowed to a crawl. A light burns behind the dirt of a window in the rustic cabin, nature having succeeded in taking over the front porch and crumbling stone chimney with vines and weeds. The window is missing a pane and a tattered curtain blows gently in the night air.

Logan shuts off the engine. "What's your plan?"

I don't technically have one. "We need proof Sylvester is alive. Let's sneak closer, and if we see him, I'll snap a photo and send it to Jones."

"And we'll let him handle it from there."

"Of course."

"Promise?"

I'm affronted. "I may take chances with ghosts, but no way I'm confronting a guy such as Sylvester."

"Good. Sometimes you worry me, and no matter how much you like Hannah or want to protect her, you could get yourself killed."

I offer a quick kiss. "I promise. No one will even know we're here."

"I doubt that," he says under his breath.

There's a throaty "meow" from the backseat and we turn in unison to find Tabby has hitchhiked. "Great," I say. She has a habit of doing this. "Stay in the car."

She gives me a bored look and begins cleaning her paw. We exit and quietly shut the doors.

The lawn is overgrown and muddy from the rain. Logan takes my arm and assists me around a rotten stack of firewood a few feet from the back door. My slippers are instantly soaked and muddy. Horrible for traction, so I appreciate his supportive embrace. We huddle under the broken window and listen.

The two woman argue, Sharon's voice growing in intensity. "I told you to stay away from him, Mother," she says. "He's going to ruin everything."

"You're worried over nothing, Sharon."

"You said the police are coming up here tomorrow. What if they find the bones? They'll know what we did."

Logan and I exchange a glance. Know what?

I fumble to tug my phone from my robe pocket and turn on my recorder app. I lift it toward the glass.

Hannah's voice quavers. "Why did you have to beat him so badly? What if he dies?"

"He won't die, but you're not marrying him. Ever. Do you hear me? I'll have you committed. Do you really think anyone believes your stupid ghost story? The whole town already thinks you're mentally unhinged and I'll take over as executor of your estate. Finally."

I feel sick to my stomach. Sharon is behind all of this.

"Ava believes me."

"That fat cow?"

I gasp and Logan slaps a hand over my mouth.

"She's not fat," Hannah defends me and I want to hug her. "Ava is lovely and kind."

Sharon makes a frustrated sound and we hear a loud thud, as though she's punched her fist into a table. "Mother! Stop already. Keeping our secret all these years has scrambled your brain. For real. I can't believe you went to her and dragged up all this old history. Why couldn't you just stay away from Burt and keep your trap shut?"

"I love him."

"He's worthless scum, just like Daddy was."

Indignation raises Hannah's voice now. "He's the nicest man I've ever met. He's always cared for us."

"Why didn't he save you back then, huh? If he was such a great guy? He knew Daddy was beating you and he did nothing. Nothing! I was the one who saved you. *Me.* And how do you repay me? By deciding to marry him and screw me out of my inheritance."

A part of me wants to rush in and defend Hannah. The other is dying to know what Sharon's talking about.

"No one could ever come between us, you know that. I'm not changing my will and you'll inherit everything when I'm gone."

"He needs to sign the prenup I gave you. That's the only way to make sure he doesn't get his hands on our money. Didn't you learn anything with Daddy?"

There's a long, pregnant pause. Logan takes out his own phone and texts someone. Probably Jones.

"Sharon, there's something I need to tell you," Hannah says quietly. "Burt is your..."

Oh boy, this won't go over well.

"My what?"

The word comes out on breathy rush. "Father."

Logan's brows disappear under his tousled bangs as he hits the send button. His eyes, deep in the shadows, are wide as he stares at me.

I nod.

Something crashes to the floor inside. "That can't be. You mean I...shot... Sly wasn't my dad?"

Hannah whimpers. "You were just a girl. You were defending me."

The revelation sinks in and it's my turn to be shocked. Snippets of Sharon telling me how much she hated the man she believed was her father, how he forced her to learn to use a gun, how she wished for a wild animal to take revenge on him...

"That monster *wasn't* my father?" Footsteps sound as she paces. The old boards squeak, her voice shaking when she stops on the other side of the window. "Why didn't you tell me?"

Hannah blubbers a few indecipherable words and Logan pulls my hand down. I'm so caught up in the story, I've forgotten she might be able to see if she looks out.

"Why didn't you divorce him?" Sharon demands. "Leave him and take us somewhere far away?"

"He would never have allowed it." Hannah sounds exasperated. "I went to a lawyer and filed the papers, but when Sylvester found out, he told me he'd kill us both if I tried to go."

She hadn't told me that.

Sharon's voice ebbs away as she returns to the table. I lift my arm again. "The police will start snooping in the morning. They'll find the bones." The words come out tight and menacing. "I'm going to prison."

More blubbering. Then, "It happened twenty years ago."

"There's no statute of limitations on murder," Logan whispers.

Sharon reiterates the same thing out loud, and then, "They'll realize I did it. Somehow, someway, they will, and I'll be tried for premeditated murder."

"But it wasn't."

"Yes, you blithering idiot, it was. I knew exactly what I was doing that day he took me out there. He wanted me to kill a deer, Mother. A poor, helpless deer."

"Oh, sweetie, I'm so sorry. But they'll never tie you to his death. How could they? I'm the only person who knows what happened."

"I either have to move the bones, or..." It's as if she isn't listening to Hannah anymore. "I know! We put the blame on Burt."

Logan is shaking his head in disgust. My arm is growing tired, but what can I do? I have to get this recorded.

"Oh no, we can't do that." Hannah makes a dismissive noise. "Burt is a sweet, loving man. He's your *father*."

Sharon rolls right over her. "You'll tell that detective Burt confessed to you. That he didn't want to marry you without telling you the truth—he killed Sylvester—and you don't know what came over you. You went ballistic and attacked him with the gun."

"But I love him, and he's innocent. I would never hurt him."

"Mother!" Sharon snap her fingers. "Focus. It's me or him."

Another long, tense silence descends. Logan and I stare at each other, holding our collective breaths and waiting.

"You really had me thinking I was being haunted by Sly's ghost." Hannah sounds sad. "Why would you do that to me?"

"If you hadn't insisted on marrying Burt, I wouldn't have had to make people think you were stark raving mad. It's always up to me to protect you from yourself. Always has been." She drops her voice. "You'd be dead if it weren't for me, and we both know it. You owe me, Mother."

"I'm so tired of all of this. I want to go back to Ava's and get some sleep."

"Not until you promise you'll go along with my plan."

"To frame Burt for Sly's death? I can't. The bones have been buried twenty years. No one's going to find them. Please, Sharon, return to your life and let me live mine."

"I was afraid you'd say that. You never learn."

Metal clanks.

"What are you doing?" Hannah asks with fear.

"What do you think?"

"I don't like this," I murmur in a hushed tone. "She's going to hurt Hannah."

Logan grabs my arm and whispers, "You promised not to interfere."

I hear the snap of the shotgun. "Sharon, please don't," Hannah says. "You're not thinking rationally. We can work this out."

"We need a distraction," I say frantically. "We can't let her harm anyone else."

A distraction appears—for me, not them. A ghost glides out from behind a tree. He's haggard, his eyes hard. "She *killed* me," he grinds out. "You have to help me. I didn't deserve to die!"

"Jury's out on that," I mumble.

Logan glances in the direction I'm staring, then back. "Ghost?"

"Sylvester," I tell him. To the apparition, I say, "I'll do what I can for you as soon as—"

Door hinges squeak behind me. Logan goes rigid, his attention rising to a spot over my head. "Ava," he says, low and foreboding. "Don't move."

"What do we have here?" Sharon's voice is frosty, yet not as cold as the metal end of the barrel she presses into my neck. "You can't keep your nose out of anything, can you? Good thing I brought extra bullets."

EIGHTEEN

I'm frozen; Logan is not. With lightning speed, he shoves me to the ground and knocks the end of the gun up into the air.

Boom! The eruption blasts my eardrums as my face hits the mud. The sticky wet soil blinds me and my phone flies behind the woodpile. I cough and sputter, ears ringing, as I attempt to get up.

My slippered feet slide and I fall again as ungracefully as an elephant on ice. I hear yelling, but it's all muffled and seems far away. As my vision clears enough for me to make out movement, I see Logan and Sharon struggling with the weapon.

Boom!

Hannah screams. I duck and cover.

A booted leg appears in my peripheral vision. *Sharon.* Reaching out, I grab it and lock my hands around her ankle.

She kicks at my head but misses. I jerk hard, using her momentum to yank her off balance. She falls next to me, screaming obscenities. Through my muffled hearing, I'm pretty sure I make out a threat to kill me.

Where's Logan?

Terrified he's been injured, I scramble around in the goop, attempting to find him, while staying out of her reach. I send a mental SOS to my guardian angel, Sherlock, Sam, and even Sage. *Help!*

Sharon grabs me by the hair and tugs. Pain sears my skull and I reach up to grasp her hand. Using the mud to her advantage, she drags me to her and wraps an arm around my neck. "Back off," she yells, and I see Logan above us, now in charge of the shotgun. The words are still muted but with her mouth near my ear, clear enough. "Or I'll break it."

"That would take a great deal of force." Persephone appears behind Logan, hovering a few feet off the ground.

Sly is watching, a frown on his face. "I don't think she can do it."

"You don't *think?*" My voice sounds too loud in my ears over the ringing. "Do something!" Logan's gaze cuts to me and the creases in his forehead deepen. "Persephone, not you," I clarify.

"She's here?" he asks.

"Behind you," I choke out as Sharon tightens her grip. "Sylvester, too."

"Shut up," she snarls in my ear. "I don't buy your act."

"I was a bad father to her," he states. "I should have done better."

I repeat what he's said. Sharon laughs. "You can't talk your way out of this. I don't care if he gets down and grovels on his ghostly knees, he's not forgiven!"

Sly shakes his head. "I am sorry."

A new ringing starts up, far away. A siren. "Police are on their way," Logan states, keeping the gun trained on her. "Let her go."

Hannah comes to stand next to us, reaching out as if to

ward him off. "Please don't shoot her. She's upset. Confused. She only wants to protect me."

I can't believe Hannah is defending her. I'm coated in mud, can't breathe, and have had it up my eyeballs with these people. "Shoot her," I gasp out. "Right between the eyes."

Hannah turns on me. "What?"

Sylvester cheers.

I kick Sharon in the shin, surprising her. She doesn't let go of my neck, but loosens her grip enough I break free with an elbow to her ribs. The slippery mud is my ally now as I roll free.

A naked woman appears off to my left, just as I hear Logan push the slide forward.

"No!" Hannah screams.

"Dinna waste your ammunition," my witchy grandmother says in her Scottish accent as she saunters past him. She flourishes a hand and Sharon grabs her neck as if choking.

Tabitha stands over her as she struggles. "Threaten my blood and incur my rage, *you blithering idiot.*"

Hannah falls to her knees beside her daughter, who's bucking around like a fish out of water. Logan grabs me and helps me stand. He keeps the gun leveled on Sharon as he asks me, "Are you okay?"

The sound of sirens grows closer. I rub my neck. "I'll live. Thank you for that. Also, I'm marrying you as soon as humanly possible. Your mother better get on board with it."

He chuckles and kisses my temple. "Sounds good to me."

"You're killing her," Hannah cries. She makes prayer hands when she glances up at my grandmother. "Please, I beg you. Don't take her from me!"

Sly floats over both of them. "Hannah needs her."

Tabitha sends her focus to me. "What say you, Ava?"

Begrudgingly, for Hannah's sake, I relent. "Let her live." I remove my muddy robe and hand it to my naked ancestor. "And cover yourself, for heaven's sake."

"Thank you," Sly says. Hannah cries over Sharon, who gasps for air.

My grandmother grins, accepts the robe, and slides it over her shoulders just in time. Blue lights skim us as Jones arrives with another cruiser. Tabitha wiggles a finger and Sharon sucks in great gulps of air, shoving her mother away when Hannah attempts to comfort her.

"Find your phone," Logan says, laying the gun on the ground and moving aside for the officer to take it.

Jones bellows as he walks toward us. "What in the name of Sweet Fanny Adams is going on here?"

Hannah cries. Sharon hunches over and wheezes. Persephone points to the ground. "It's here."

I scramble to the phone and hold it out to Jones, realizing my robe is now lying on the ground behind the woodpile. A marmalade cat rubs against my leg. "It's all recorded," I tell him. "Sharon shot Sylvester and Hannah covered it up. The bones are buried on this property. It was Sharon who attacked Burt."

For a moment, Jones stares at all of us, befuddled, then he directs those with him to take Sharon and Hannah into custody.

I play back the recording and he sighs deeply. "You two are a pain in my backside, you know that?"

"We just proved Sylvester Grady was murdered and got you the proof of who committed the crime."

"Yeah, yeah, yeah. Go home, Fantome, and send me a copy of that recording. I'll handle things from here, and I want a formal statement from both of you first thing in the morning. See you at the station."

Tabby is waiting with Persephone in the car. "That was exciting," the angel says, stroking Tabby's fur.

"Was Sly hanging around here all this time?" I ask.

"He crossed as soon as he died," she assures me. "He only came back tonight because he knew Sharon was dangerous."

Logan heads for home and I reach over and clasp one of his hands. "You were amazing tonight, you know that?"

His smile is rueful. "Like Tabitha, I don't take kindly to anyone threatening you."

I need a hot shower and for my ears to stop ringing. My heart hurts for Hannah, even if she did screw things up. "Hannah is going to need a good lawyer."

Logan glances at me, reading my thoughts. "You can't be serious."

"Sylvester was abusive. Sharon was just a kid, trying to protect her mother, and then Hannah had to cover up what she did. It's not right, but I understand why she did it." I would bet Mama would have done the same for me, although I can't imagine us ever being in such a situation. "I know she's guilty, but a jury might go easier on her if she has an attorney who can present it as a mother trying to shield her young daughter from a monster."

Logan drives for a while in silence, still holding my hand. Finally, he gives my fingers a squeeze. "I'll see what I can do."

NINETEEN

After a shower, I succumb to an exhaustive sleep filled with nightmares. When I finally give up around five, I find Logan working in the living room, journals, files, and law books scattered across the coffee table. His computer rests on his lap.

He glances up as I enter. "Can't sleep?"

Everything comes crashing back, the lingering nightmares more vivid than I care to admit. Ghosts, blood, irises. Silver cords, all connected to me and draining me of my energy. Young girls wielding weapons.

Tears sting my eyes, and all I can do is shake my head. "Hannah trusted me. I feel like I failed her."

He sets the laptop down and removes his glasses. The circles under his eyes suggest he's been up all night. "I've contacted a college acquaintance who specializes in criminal law, and chiefly works with women who've been in abusive relationships. She's excellent and I'm sure she'll take the case."

"Thank you."

He studies me. "The trust thing runs both ways, you know. You trusted Hannah to tell you the truth and she didn't."

Withheld information is more like it, but that makes no difference at the moment. "I keep feeling the barrel of that gun pressed against my neck."

He opens his arms and I go to him, sinking into his welcome embrace. I rest my head against his chest, listening to his heart. I'm lucky to be here, lucky nothing happened to him, either. I couldn't live with myself if it had. His heartbeat, strong and steady lulls me to sleep.

That morning, Rosie finds us spooned together on the couch, finally getting the rest we need. When I wake, she's waving freshly brewed coffee under my nose. I'm stiff and achy, and the brew is the best thing I've tasted in forever. Sam's longing to be human again in order to eat sends a pang of regret through me. It's easy to understand at the moment when the warm, good-smelling drink feels like a lifesaver.

"Rough night?" Rosie asks as Logan sits up, yawns and rubs his face with his hands.

I hand him the cup so he can have a sip. "Awful."

She heads for her desk. "I heard about the Gradys. So there's no ghost?"

I almost wish there were. I stand and stretch. "Nope. I'll go clean up and be ready for our first appointment."

Jenn bursts through the front door, Lia with her. "We heard what happened!" Lia rushes toward me, looking me over from head to toe. "They found the bones of that guy this morning. Did you talk to his spirit? Is that how you found him? This is so cool. Wait 'til I tell everybody I'm friends with a ghost-whisperer!"

My head throbs with an instant headache. "If you're staying, I'll put you both to work."

"That's what I'm here for," Jenn assures me. She studies

Logan and the mess spread out on the coffee table. "You know, you could use an assistant, too," she says.

He gathers his files and kisses my cheek. "What I need is a shower. I'll catch up with you later."

"Can someone feed Moxley and the cats for me?" It's not actual work, but today, I need all the help I can get.

"I will," Lia says. "I can walk the dog, too."

"You're hired," I tell her. "And the case with Hannah isn't closed yet." It's not a total lie. "We can't discuss it with anyone, understand?"

Some of her excitement drains away but she makes a motion as if she's locking her lips and throwing away the key. "Can I write it down in my journal?"

"As long as you keep the details confidential."

After dressing and doing my hair and makeup, I return downstairs to find everything humming along fine without me. "Detective Jones phoned," Rosie says. "I left the message on your desk. Burt is doing okay. Jones asked that you call him back."

My stomach growls and I smell something baking in the kitchen. For a brief heartbeat, fear spikes in my belly, but it's not Trysta in my kitchen. It's Sage.

"I made a coffeecake," she says without glancing at me as she pulls it bubbling from the oven. "Heard about your troubles last night. Thought you could use a hand this morning."

I grab a drink refill and drop into a chair. "Sylvester was not haunting her. I had it all wrong."

She dishes up the steaming gooeyness and puts a bowl of it in front of me. "Sounds like you didn't have all the facts."

I toy with the food, blowing on a spoonful of cherries and cake to cool it. Daddy texted earlier to apologize for misleading me with his theory on Sly. I've already told him not to worry about it. "It's got me thinking about Trysta, though. What if she's not what we think she is? What if she isn't using the men to stay here in the flesh, but the other way around?"

Sage sits across from me. "What do you mean?"

The coffeecake is delicious but so hot, I gingerly take another bite. "Those spirits. What if they aren't really dead? At least not yet."

"You've lost me."

"Let me finish this and I'll show you something." I point at the bowl. "This is amazing, by the way. I didn't know you could cook."

She wiggles her fingers and grins. "Magic."

Logan joins us and devours half the treat while I show Sage one of the videos from the previous night. "See here when Charles and Trysta arrived? She's hidden from the camera under the umbrella, but you can spot the ghosts connected to her."

"Cool," Sage murmurs, angling the phone for a better view of the screen. She replays the clip, stops it, and enlarges the frame. "It's like she's a horse pulling them along."

"Exactly, but what if they're pushing her, rather than her pulling?"

Sage and Logan glance at me, questioning looks on both of their faces. "I don't get it," Logan says.

"It's a symbiotic relationship, right?" I point to the men. "Daddy told me Larry Lambert, her adoptive father, is still in a coma. What if the others are, too? What if they've hooked themselves to her in order to stay alive?"

"But she's a ghost," Sage says.

"Is she though?" I pick a new clip. "Look here when she's fleeing the house after our confrontation. Does she look like one to you?"

Sage freezes a frame and zooms in on Trysta's backside.

"No, but I thought that's why she was using the men's energy—to stay corporeal."

"I tore off her necklace last night. I thought it held pieces of the men and that she was using those to stay connected to them. Unfortunately, she didn't turn into a spectral before she grabbed it back."

"Residual energy," Sage counters. "She still had reserves, that's all."

"Are you sure? She felt so real when I held onto her. And did you notice the ghosts stayed out of the house? In that video, they were suspended out there on the porch. She's told me several times that she feels lighter and happier when she's here. I thought it was because she's crushing on Logan, but now I wonder if it's because unwanted spirits can't cross the threshold, but she can because she's not a ghost."

Sage grins at Logan. "She's crushing on *you?* Isn't she marrying your brother?"

"Focus," I tell her. "Do you think it's possible? She was hit by lightning when she was a kid. Her adoptive father, who I believe is one of those attached to her, was there. He was supposedly struck, as well. Could their energies have gotten entangled somehow? He's still in a coma, and could be using her to stay alive, even though he can't wake up."

"Okay," Sage says, tapping her finger idly against the phone. "Table that for a moment. How did the other two men end up connected to her? She can't have been hit three times."

Never say never. "I'm still working on that." If my guardian angel would actually tell me things... Of course, then I'd end up like Sherlock—in trouble with the Big Guy, or whoever is running the afterlife. "But if she's human, she still needs my help. I have to remove those cords."

Logan's college acquaintance returns his call and he bails.

Sage rises, telling me she's meeting Bis for an impromptu breakfast downtown. "You're not cooking for him?" I ask.

"He hasn't earned it yet."

I'm surprisingly pleased that I have.

After she leaves, I contact Daddy. "Any more on Mabel?"

"Actually, I was going to call you. I heard about last night."

"I'm fine, but extremely disappointed your theory wasn't correct. It would have been better than the truth."

"I was way off base about that whole thing. Solving mysteries is a shell game. Sometimes, you lose sight of the ball and pick the wrong cup. I'm glad you're okay, though."

"Logan saved my life."

"So I heard. We owe him big time. You two still getting hitched this weekend?"

"No." My heart aches with the reality of it. "For now, we're holding off."

"Okay, well, if you change your mind, your mother and I will be there, wherever, whenever." He clears his throat and I hear papers shuffling. "About Mabel. There's not much that I could uncover. There's census data, documentation of a couple hospital visits, and some school records. That's it."

"What was she in the hospital for? The lightning strike?"

"You guessed it. According to a write up in the local paper where she lived, when she was eleven, she was talking on a landline phone and got a jolt when lightning struck a metal antenna on the roof of their house. The electricity was conducted through the cord and left her paralyzed for several days. She saw a doctor a few times after that for various odd abnormalities."

"The doctor she eventually married?"

"Yep. Frederickson. He took a strong interest in her case and wrote three papers on her. I found one of them online."

"What kind of abnormalities?"

More shuffling. "Says here she claimed she could see and talk to the dead."

Gooseflesh covers my arms. My mind whirls. "That's what started all of this."

"So Mabel was a medium like you?"

She is nothing like me, but I discover to my surprise I feel sorry for her. I'm sure folks in the sixties were no kinder to her then, than they are now when they discover you can see ghosts. "Was she ever put in a mental institute?"

"Dr. Frederickson recommended psychiatric help, but I haven't found any records that she received it. She dropped out of school at sixteen and if I'm right..." There's a pause. "Yep, he married her when she was eighteen."

Too weird. "Okay, Daddy, anything else?"

"That's it. Do you need me to keep digging?"

"I believe I have what I need for now." At least, I hope I do. "Thanks."

"I know you're always careful with spirits, but watch your back, okay? I have a bad feeling about this one."

Me, too, I think. *Me, too.*

TWENTY

G host or human? I still can't decide.

I work with Rosie handling our morning appointment. It's a lone women, Mary Johansen, who's marrying her school sweetheart in a private ceremony in the backyard next week. We have all the supplies and she has her mother's dress to wear. All we're doing today is going over the final itinerary.

I walk her into the yard, where she sniffs deeply and smiles at the pink roses grouped around the gazebo. "It's going to be perfect," she says. "I'm so happy to be having a simple ceremony in nature."

"Aunt Willa had a green thumb, that's for sure. It's my dream to marry here, too."

She faces me. Her grandmother's spirit hovers near us. "You've snagged the most eligible bachelor in the state. I'd think you'd want a grand wedding with all the bells and whistles."

My heart is full as I look at the pretty flowers, the white gazebo where dozens of couples have said their vows, and the homestead down the hill, where generations of my family have lived. "This is what makes me happy," I tell her. "I love a good party, don't get me wrong, but this?" I motion at the roses and trees. "This is more my style."

"You should follow your heart."

Her grandmother smiles. "She's right, you know."

Around lunch time, Logan and I sit down with Jones at the police station. He takes us into a bare room with only a table and two chairs to record our statements. When I'm done giving mine, he turns off the camera and scribbles on his legal pad. "Did Hannah Grady actually believe the ghost of her dead husband was haunting her?"

I don't want to add to the idea he and many others have regarding her mental state. "She came to me to discuss her birthday, that's all."

He scowls and glances up to meet my eyes. "Was there a ghost?"

A generic question that he hopes will give him more insight. "Ghosts are everywhere, detective. You'll have to be more specific. If you're asking if there was one trying to harm Hannah, I can tell you I didn't witness any."

This seems to satisfy him. After all, he can't put that in a report without calling his own sanity into question. He escorts Logan and I to the lobby and we leave, picking up lunch from Queenie's. We find Helen waiting for us when we arrive back at The Wedding Chapel. Lia is telling her about ghost hunting as she clicks away at the computer on my desk.

"Hello, Mother." Logan kisses her cheek. "I didn't know you'd be stopping by to see me today."

Helen smiles at him, barely glances at me. "I've come to discuss a few things with Ava."

"We were going to have lunch," he tells her. "Would you like to join us?"

"I've eaten." She dismisses us with a hand. "Go enjoy your food."

"The software is installed," Lia says to me. "You need to download the app and we'll link it to your phone."

She resumes her story without missing a beat. Helen sits immobile, listening intently.

Rosie nods as we pass, her desk phone tucked between ear and shoulder as she takes an order from a customer. Jenn is nowhere to be seen, but humming is coming from the storage room in back, and I assume she's sorting through decorations for Mary's wedding.

"Can't you do something?" Logan whispers, once we're in the kitchen and out of earshot. "About Lia and her ghost talk?"

"I need food before I deal with your mother. Besides, Lia is a kid. I can use that excuse if your mother is upset." Which I don't believe she is, considering our last discussion and the fact she's still entertaining Lia's elaborate discussion at the moment.

He pulls the containers from the bag. He still looks tired, but is dressed in a snappy gray suit that makes my mouth water. "That might work."

With his good looks, he's always handsome, but I think about what Mary said regarding him being the most eligible bachelor in the state. Her comment to follow my heart rings in my ears. "Helen did offer to help with Hannah when I suspected Sly was haunting her. She isn't as closed minded about this stuff as she acts."

He snickers. "Mother always has an angle. I love her, but you've been warned. Don't let your guard down. She'll eat you for dinner."

"Don't worry." I may have an angle, too, depending on what this visit is about. "I'll handle it."

His contact is going to take Hannah's case and that makes me happy. Jones wouldn't discuss specifics, but he hinted at the fact he suspected the prosecutor's office would look bad if they tried to crucify Hannah due to the circumstances. Sharon is another story, since she pulled the trigger, but being an eleven-year-old at that time might help her situation.

By the time we've wolfed down our sandwiches, Logan has to rush off to a meeting. I clean up the mess and go see why my future mother-in-law is here.

Helen waits patiently until Lia finishes installing the app on my phone and giving me a brief tutorial on how to use it to track expenses, then she asks the girl to give us privacy and closes the stately double doors.

I sit back in my chair and prep my armor. The look on her face suggests I'm going to need it. "Did you want to talk about the engagement party?" I ask.

She sits straighter and peers down her nose at me. "What I want to discuss is you."

"Oh?" This ought to be good. "If this is about last night, Logan and I feared for Hannah's life. We had to follow her. I'm sorry he was put in danger, but—"

"That's not why I'm here, but you're lucky nothing happened to my son because of your meddling." Her eyes, so much like Logan's, are hard and unforgiving. Whatever camaraderie we shared the other night is gone. "What I want to know is: why did you attack Trysta last night, and how exactly do you plan to make it up to her?"

I wasn't expecting that. "I didn't attack her." The need to defend myself when Trysta is the problem galls me. I feel no need to keep up the ruse any longer and pretend. "There are things about her you don't know. She's bad news, Helen, and I'm trying to get the bottom of it before Charles makes a horrible mistake."

"Oh, please. If this is some nonsense about what happened with her father all those years ago, I already know."

Nonsense? "You know about the lightning strike?"

She barely deigns to nod, as if I don't deserve an answer.

"She's traumatized, and yes, she seeks out daddy figures to fill that role, but she's not a bad person."

I eye the matriarch of the Cross dynasty. She probably feels some odd bond with a self-made tycoon like Larry Lambert. "You had a background check run on her, didn't you?"

"I did." She brushes at non-existent lint on her pale lemon skirt. "I confronted her about what happened when she was a girl, and she explained it to me. Not only was she once more an orphan after the accident, and was thrown back into the foster system, she was scarred physically from the strike. Every time she looks at her leg, she sees her stepfather. In her young mind, she believed she should have been able to save him."

"She's a ghost." My next statement is pure conjecture, but I'm willing to run with it. "She died that night."

Helen is taken aback. "No, she didn't. She fell into a brief coma that mimicked death, that's all. The doctors told her she was lucky."

"It wasn't luck, though." I haven't had time to look this up, but Persephone pops in and nods as if my guess is correct. "There was some bizarre exchange of energy. Her adoptive father went into the coma, not Trysta. Or should I call her Stacey? The lightning stopped her heart, I'm betting on it, and somehow he brought her back to life."

"I'm beginning to believe you're as unstable as Trysta claims." Helen stands, the full weight of her anger crashing over me. "I've had misgivings about you marrying Logan all along, but this is more than I can overlook. Leave her be. She's been through enough, and stop spreading ridiculous rumors about her."

"Rumors?" I haven't talked to anyone but Daddy in regards to Trysta. "Helen, you know me. You know I can see and hear spirits. By all accounts, Trysta is dead, or close to it, and she's using your son to keep her in human form. I don't make this stuff up!"

"This is nonsense." She walks to the door and slides it open. Rosie, Jenn, and Lia all jump away, caught in the act of eavesdropping. She doesn't bother to call them on it. "You better watch yourself," she warns me. "Or I'll make sure you never become Mrs. Logan Cross."

She takes one step out of the room and I push to my feet. "Are you threatening me?"

Whirling around, she points a finger like a gun at my chest. "I know all about your secret wedding in the backyard. Do you think you can defy me, Ava? I'll crush you like a pineapple, if you dare try."

For a moment, I'm frozen in place. I watch as she jerks the front door open. It bangs against the coat hooks and the eyes of the other women, gawking unapologetically, swing to me.

I don't take threats lightly, nor do I care for folks who toss them out and then run. Calling on all of my patience, I follow her outside, determined to catch up. The secret wedding is the real issue here, not Trysta. "Helen, wait. Come back inside and let's finish discussing this."

"I have nothing further to say to you until you apologize to Trysta."

The ghost herself watches from behind a window inside the bakery. I swear she's smiling. "I realize I've blindsided you with all of this, most especially the wedding," I tell Helen. "It was not our intent to defy your wishes regarding the ceremony, but I've dreamed all my life of marrying in Aunt Willa's backyard garden in June. I'm a romantic at heart. However, your wishes are actually what Logan and I have been focused on. We want you to have your ideal ceremony for him, as well. The two of us committing ourselves to each other this week with a simple observance to fulfill mine, while still holding the big

Cross extravaganza in the fall to fulfill yours, seems like a satisfactory compromise." I give her a big smile. "Doesn't it?"

The corners of her eyes narrow. "Is that the lie you told yourself so you'd feel better about going behind my back? Is that what you told Logan to ease his conscious and go along with your plan?"

"It's not a lie and I didn't need to ease anyone's conscious. We're two adults who wish to marry and we were attempting to make you happy, even at the expense of forcing me to compromise what I want. Did you stop for one minute and consider that, Helen? *I* am the bride. It's *my* wedding."

She blanches. "You're a selfish woman."

As she starts to walk away again, I step in front of her. *I will not rise to her taunts.* The only person here who's being selfish isn't me, and if we're going to share Logan, then we must come to an agreement. "I've done everything you've asked of me. I saved Logan from your family curse and I love him more than life itself. He's saved my life, more than once, and I'm indebted to him. The only person in this scenario who I actually care about making happy is him. So let's strike a deal. Let's ask Logan what *he* wants and we'll abide by whatever he chooses." I take a deep breath and unclench my hands. It's challenging, but I produce another smile. "What do you say?"

Her perfectly arched brows hit her hairline. "Let Logan decide?"

She makes it sound as if it's a preposterous idea.

It's not. "You love him as much as I do, right? You want him to be happy, don't you?"

Her eyes snap, hearing the challenge in my voice. She senses I've trapped her, and Helen Cross is not one to be trapped. "Apologize to Trysta."

"And you'll speak to Logan about his preference for the ceremony?"

It kills her but she nods. I move sideways so she can continue to her car. An idea strikes and I call to her before she can climb inside. "Come with me."

"What?"

"I want to apologize to her right now." I point to the window where Trysta hurriedly ducks out of sight. "Come with me."

Sensing this is another trap, she shakes her head. "I have business to attend to."

"Then I'll wait until you can be present. When can you put me on your schedule?"

Huffing, she tosses her purse onto the passenger seat and shuts the car door. "Fine. Let's get this over with."

I was nearly killed last night. I have no desire to wait until October to make my vows to Logan. I want to tell her that, but a deal is a deal. I know what Logan will choose when asked. Maybe Helen suspects it, too. Either way, it's time to deal with Trysta.

Helen marches across the street. I follow, knowing the ghost is watching and hoping she's also panicking at the development.

Secretly, I smile to myself. *Persephone*, I call telepathically. *You don't want to miss this.*

She appears beside me instantly, which is such a rare thing. "What are you doing?" my guardian angel asks.

"Ghost whispering," I say. "What else?"

TWENTY-ONE

Before I get two feet closer to the bakery, Sage rolls up and parks. Her window is down and she points at the passenger seat. "Got your cat."

As she gets out, Tabby jumps down and peers at me.

"Bad kitty," I tell her, wagging my finger. "What are you doing hitch-hiking with Sage?"

"No harm done. I like her." She starts to get back in her vehicle as Tabby turns up her nose and prances to the sidewalk.

"Wait." I rush to the car. "I need you to come with me."

"Where?"

I nod toward the bakery. "Across the street."

Sage eyes the place, then me. "Why?"

"Play along." I grab her arm and drag her with me. "I need moral support."

"I don't like this," Persephone says.

Sam appears. "It is ill advised to walk into your enemy's camp."

Tabby joins us, now that Sam is present. Helen is at the door of the business, and she looks back with a raised brow.

"Be right there," I call, then hook my arm through Sage's and lower my voice. "Everyone come with me. Persephone, it's time you come forth with the truth about her—she's a ghost, isn't she?"

Her hair is bright pink and she wears a black jumpsuit, studded with pink sequins. "I already told you she was."

"Sam, can you speak to the ones who are attached to her?"

He straightens his waistcoat. "For your sake? I shall try. What is it you wish me to say?"

"Find out who they are, if you can. I think one is a stepfather and another a husband. Not sure about the third. See if you can decipher if they're forcing her to do their bidding, or she's the one pulling the strings."

He nods.

"Are you talking to ghosts?" Sage asks.

"My grandfather and my guardian angel." Tabby rubs my ankles, as if asking what she should do. I bend down so I'm closer to her eye level. "Help me find the necklace, or whatever else may be keeping her tied to them."

Tabby leads the way and we join Helen on the porch. "The cat can't come inside," she scolds. "It's a bakery."

Tabby hisses and Helen jumps back. Trysta swings open the door, fake surprise on her face. "Well, look who's here. I wasn't expecting guests."

Helen smiles, cool as a cucumber, and motions at me. "Ava wishes to apologize for her demeaning behavior last night."

Trysta's eyes land on me. Her hand goes into the pocket of her apron. Vanilla and cinnamon tease my nose. "Is that so?"

I force a friendly smile. Tabby slips by her, unnoticed. " May we come in?"

"I really wish I could chat but I'm in the middle of baking. Only two days until the grand opening, and I have so much to do! I'm sure you understand."

Sage peers over her shoulder. "We'd like to help."

Good one.

Trysta appears baffled by such a suggestion. Persephone floats right through her and she recoils. Sam passes through the wall, and she stiffens, head jerking to the left to follow his movements. "That's quite generous, but not at all necessary."

"I've brought my friend, Sage." I lift Sage's hand, hitting on my own good idea. "She can repair the necklace."

"I can?"

I covertly step on her foot.

She winces and then brightens. "Oh, right. Yes, I can fix it."

The shirt Trysta wears buttons up to her neck and I can't see if she's wearing it. From the way she keeps her hand in her pocket, I suspect it's there instead. "No need. I'm taking it to the jeweler tomorrow."

"But you don't have time, do you?" Helen asks. "Getting ready for the opening and all?"

Flustered, she flaps the other hand. "Charles is taking it for me." She realizes the contradiction and tries to cover it with a laugh and some misdirection. "He really is the best, isn't he, Mrs. Cross? Him and Logi both."

Helen's already rigid posture becomes more taut. "Logan. He doesn't care for nicknames."

Neither do you. At least we agree on that.

The hand finally comes out of the pocket to worry the other. "Oh, he never seems to mind."

"Can I get some cupcakes to take to my sisters?" Sage asks.

She's good at this. "Oh, I bet they'd love some." I nod vigorously. "And you could take Trysta's business cards to hand out at your shop. Help her spread the word."

Trysta turns to look over her shoulder, and since I can no longer see Sam, I wonder if she's still tracking him or sensing he and Persephone are talking to her ghost friends.

Helen, tired of standing on the porch, brushes past her. "Young lady, it's rude to deny an apology."

Sage and I exchange a look and enter as Trysta hops out of the way and makes a small squeak in her throat. "All's forgiven," she says to me, even though her gaze is pure anger. "No need for any formal apology."

Inside, we all stop and peer around, astonishment evident on everyone's face. She has transformed Logan's former reception area into a pastel dream. Candy-striped wall paper, white chair rails, and cartoon cupcakes line the walls. Two large cases filled with the goodies fan out from the center register. Behind those are shelves with rows of more confections in every color and loaded with frosting, sprinkles, cherries, nuts, and more.

"Whoa," Sage says, gawking. "This is...something."

Helen gives an appreciative bob of her head. "You've transformed the place."

The round, white tables are stationed every few feet around the perimeter. Stools fashioned like cupcakes, with pink, yellow, and purple pillows suggesting frosting, sit around them.

She's installed a swinging metal door to the back, once Logan's office. Persephone peers through the round window but shakes her head. I make a face and raise my hands. *What?*

"Do you like it?" Trysta asks no one in particular. "It's cheery, right?"

"It's beautiful," I say, truthfully. I catch a glimpse of Sam behind the counter, and the three ghosts he's speaking with flicker in and out. "Definitely not what I expected with a name like Killer Cupcakes."

"I dig the name," Sage comments.

I step on her foot again and she elbows me in return.

"I was torn between that and Death by Cupcake." Trysta looks almost wistful, but the subject reminds me she's poisoned my friend and is not a nice person, no matter how much pastel and sugar she layers on.

"You seem fixated with death and violence, Stacey."

All eyes turn to me.

She acts shocked, but I see her eyes harden. "Why do you keep calling me that?"

"Dr. Murphy Frederickson," Sam says, hovering near my arm. "Her doctor and husband. One of them, anyway. Alvin DeCote was Mabel's second husband."

"Is Larry Lamont one of the spirits?"

"What?" Trysta exclaims.

"Ava," Helen warns.

"You are correct." Sam looks pleased. "All three men are in comas, it seems."

Persephone floats in, eating a cupcake. "Holy kittens, Ava. These are good."

Helen, Trysta, and Sage gape at the pink confection floating in the air. Persephone seems to enjoy freaking them out and dances around with it. "There is a blood contract in place between the entities," she tells me. "I can't say more than that."

"Tell me about the contract." I face Trysta. "Between you, Frederick, Alvin, and Larry."

She sticks out both hands as if to ward me off. "No, no, no. You can't know..." Catching herself, she glances at Helen and gives a whimper. "She's doing it again, Miss Helen. You're my witness. Ava is crazy!"

Before I can pin her down and finish our talk, Jenn bursts in, out of breath. "Help!"

I grab her arm. "What's wrong?"

"Rosie." She sucks in a gulp of air. She acts like she's run a sprint, but she's still carrying baby weight and the dash across the street is enough to wind her. "She needs you."

I go the door. Rosie is on the sidewalk, clutching her stomach and making a face. "Oh, lord."

"What's wrong?" Helen asks.

I move by Jenn and race down the steps. There's a puddle on the sidewalk. "Her water broke."

TWENTY-TWO

"Do not have that baby before I get you to the—"

From the passenger seat, Rosie grips the gold cross on her collarbone. "Ahhhgghhh." A string of curses follow.

I press the accelerator and pass a truck. A horn blares. "The baby isn't due yet."

Rosie huffs, her practiced breathing technique causing her lips to pucker. "Guess this one is strong-willed...like me. She's ready...to meet the world."

"Hurry," Persephone goads from the back seat, "or you'll be delivering her right here in this vehicle."

"You're a lot of help," I grumble.

My human passenger has braced her hands on the dashboard and is gripping it so hard, her nails are leaving imprints in it. "Whaaat?"

"Sorry, that was meant for Persephone."

"She's..."—*huff, huff, huff*—"here?"

"Moral support." It's for me, rather than her, but Rosie doesn't need to know that.

I've left Jenn in charge at The Chapel, and she's called

Rosie's husband to let him know I'm taking her to the hospital. Lia insisted she'd stay and help Jenn with the afternoon client, so I put her in charge of Fern and the other animals. I told her not to talk about ghosts in front of anyone. She reluctantly agreed. When I drove off, Helen still stood on the porch of the bakery.

Rosie begins working her maternity pants loose. "I have to get these off."

Whoa. "I don't think that's a good idea."

"She's going to have the baby in this car," Persephone states.

I wrench around. "Do you know that or are you guessing?"

Rosie releases a huge sigh as her waistband unfurls. "Know what?"

My fingers shake and I grip the steering wheel harder. "Nothing. You know Persephone and her ability to manipulate details."

The guardian angel mocks me from the back. "You say that like I'm the difficult one in this relationship. I can disappear right now, you know. Leave you to deliver that baby on your own."

"Is my daughter"—*huff, huff, huff*—"okay?"

"Yes," I reassure my friend. "She wasn't talking about the baby. She was referring to...Trysta."

Sam pops in beside the angel, bringing a gust of cool air and the scent of the homestead. "You are a persnickety one, aren't you, Seph?"

The temperature in the vehicle drops another few degrees as she raises her voice. "Don't call me that."

"I beg your forgiveness. Sherlock uses the nickname, and you seem fine with it."

A quick glance in the rearview shows me her sneer. "Sherlock can take his nickname and shove it right up his—"

"Persephone!" I glance between Rosie and the road before I glare at her. "Behave yourself. You're an angel, for heaven's sake."

"Drive faster," she instructs, shifting to look at the passing scenery.

"I'm going as fast as I can and still be safe."

"I know," Rosie says, through her breathing. "I'm scared, Ava."

I reach for her hand to squeeze it. "Everything will be fine."

Her dark eyes meet mine with alarm. "I need to push."

"No!" I take my hand back, needing it to steady myself as I take a wild turn to hit the highway leading to the hospital. "No pushing!"

My guardian angel chuckles. "You can't stop nature."

Unfortunately, she's right. Before we get another mile, Rosie braces her feet and howls. The shriek makes me flinch and wish I could cover my ears. When the contraction passes, she screams at me, "She's coming! The baby is coming now!"

"What should I do?"

"Pull over," Persephone says, without an ounce of anxiety. "Get her in the backseat."

"She's in labor. I can't move her."

Rosie spreads her knees wider. "I need...to...lie down."

Taking a moment to breathe myself, I careen to the shoulder of the road. The ground is all dirt and we hit a pothole, jarring both of us. "Sorry," I say when she groans.

"Please help me." *Huff, huff, huff.* "I can't believe this is...happening."

"That makes two of us." I park and rush around the front of the car to her side. Together, we manage to pivot her body so her feet are on the ground. She braces her hands on the frame to steady herself, and I open the rear door. "Are you sure the baby won't, you know, slide out when I move her?" I whisper to Persephone.

The angel laughs, floating out of the vehicle. "Not unless she pushes at that exact moment."

Good to know. Wedging my hands under Rosie's arms, I grunt as I help her stand. Her weight, combined with the baby's, causes muscles I didn't even know I had to strain.

She has to pause and catch her breath before we take a step. The process to get her the three feet around the open door is slow and arduous. As we take the final move, she grows angry. "Why did I want another child? I hate labor." *Huff, huff, huff.* "I'm going to kill Matt for doing this to me. Do you hear me?"

"I would, too," I agree. After this, I'm never having kids. Hope Logan is okay with that. Her legs are bowed out and I'm still scared to death the baby will fall out on its head and have brain damage. "Use that anger and let's get you right... over...here."

Plunk, she drops to the seat, her body losing its balance. She rolls onto her back, her bent legs going with her and *whoa.* Yep, that little girl is nearly here. "I know nothing about giving birth, but I believe she's—what's the term?—crowning?"

"I know!" Her voice is tight with pain. "I have to push!"

"Oh jeez, oh jeez, oh jeez. What do I do?"

A car rolls up behind us and Helen gets out. "Please tell me she's not having the child here."

"Arrrggghhh," Rosie cries.

"Get in," Helen orders me. "I'll drive."

She half pushes me in beside my friend, and Rosie grips my hand so tightly, I nearly cry along with her.

"Don't push," Helen calls over her shoulder as she navigates us onto the highway and slams down the gas pedal. "We're nearly there. Hang on a little longer."

We bump and careen as she pushes my vehicle to speeds it

has never experienced since I've owned it. The rest of the ride probably only lasts another ten minutes, but it feels like an eternity with Rosie screaming at the top of her lungs and crushing my bones.

Matt has called ahead and staff in scrubs meet us at the ER entrance with a gurney. Rosie refuses to turn loose of my hand as they maneuver her out of the seat and onto it. I contort my body to stay with her, unable to break free from her vise-like grip.

Running alongside as they wheel her to the elevator, a doctor informs me I can ride up to the maternity floor with her, but I'm not allowed in the delivery room.

"Gosh, that's a shame," I say without a trace of disappointment. I may never be able to use my hand again as it's now numb, but the torture is nothing compared to what Rosie is going through. She seems to waver between cursing all of us, and especially Matt, in Spanish, and drifting into la-la land. "Her husband should be here soon."

Inside, she nearly sits up when a contraction hits. They're so close, I've stopped timing them. "Push! I have to push!" she screams.

"Don't," three of the team reply.

Renewed agony runs from my fingers up my arm as she crushes it once more. Her dark eyes are wild and filled with a plea. Sweat trickles down her face as she stares up at me. "I need to...*push*," she grounds out.

Persephone appears. The elevator dings and the doors open to the third floor. "She'll be okay," my angel says. "The doctors will take care of her."

I nod at Rosie. "Do what you have to do," I whisper.

With a roar that stops all activity on the floor, she curls forward, leveraging herself with my support, and the next thing we know, surprise! The baby is born.

· · ·

A FEW HOURS LATER, I'm in the waiting room, Helen with me. Logan texted and I filled him in on the harrowing event, giving his mother—who was within earshot—all the credit for getting us here in the nick of time. Jenn and Lia let me know the afternoon appointment went fine. and Jenn not only booked a party from it, the woman requested a consult for an anniversary gown, designed in the pattern of my ritzy Bellamy. My mind automatically sees it in a frosted champagne, rather than white, and I make a note to discuss it with Gloria.

Matt enters holding his son's hand. Mikey is all smiles, swinging their connected arms. "I'm a big brother!"

Matt is grinning, too. "Rosie wants to see you." He glances at Helen. "You as well, Mrs. Cross."

We follow him to room 317 and I find my friend's face lit with joy as she holds the newborn. "We've decided on a name and I thought you two should be the first to hear it."

Helen and I exchange a look. "Iselina?" I venture, since it's one we discussed. Rosie's deceased abuela, Ysela, begged for her to name the girl after her, but Rosie had other ideas.

She turns the swaddled child so we can view her face. Her eyes are slits, her cheeks soft as a peach. "Ladies, I would like you to meet Avalen Sela Rodriguez." She pauses, smiling at us. "We combined Avalon and Helen, what do you think?"

"That's beautiful," Helen says, touching the blanket. "I'm honored."

I'm speechless. Rosie's eyes sparkle. My injured hand aches but it's so worth it right now to see how happy she is, and to have her daughter named after me. "Are you sure?"

She rolls her eyes and swats my arm. "You two got me to

the hospital. I have no doubt you would have delivered this baby on your own, if you'd had to, Ava. Yes, we're sure."

I stroke one chubby hand, tiny and perfect. "I don't know what to say. It's the nicest thing anyone's ever done for me."

Helen, surprisingly, touches my arm in the shared moment.

Matt hefts Mikey up onto the bed and he sits on his knees at Rosie's side. "I'm a big brother," he repeats, hooking a thumb at his chest.

"Yes, you are," Helen says. "Being the older sibling comes with important responsibilities. Are you ready for them?"

He puffs out his chest. "You bet."

We leave the family and locate my car. Both of us are tired, and although we've just bonded because of a birth, we're edgy with each other over Trysta. I'm nearly to Helen's abandoned vehicle on the side of the road before she speaks. "What do you mean about Trysta being a ghost? She's as real as you or I."

I try to bring my mind around to the issue, but when I attempt to tell her what I've uncovered, along with how I can spot the ghosts attached to her, it comes out disjointed. "I know it sounds impossible, but I'm sure she's only walking around on this physical plane because of the energy she's sucking off those ghosts and your son."

Helen sits rigid in her seat, silent, even after I pull in across from her car. She stares out at the falling darkness. "Why do these things keep happening to my family?"

I think about Hannah and Sharon. About my own family's run-ins with killer spirits. "It's not your fault," I assure her. "There are a lot of strange things in this world that most folks never realize. A lot of earthbound ghosts, too. I believe Trysta, like many of them, refuses to move on."

"I'm not saying I believe you, but I'll try to keep an open mind about it. I may have turned a blind eye to some of her more, shall we say, undesirable attributes, because she makes

Charles happy. I haven't seen him like this since, well...ever. He loves her."

I have no answer to that, no platitudes. Helen leaves me without a goodbye and I wait until she drives away before I head for home.

The sun has set by the time I arrive. No lights are on. Did Logan have a late meeting and forgot to mention it? Perhaps he's in his office engrossed in his latest case and hasn't noticed night has fallen. I can't wait to tell him about the baby.

Across the street, the bakery is ablaze with lights. It's not the best time to confront Trysta, yet, I feel an urge to see what she's up to.

Standing by my vehicle, debating whether to confront her again, Persephone appears at the side of the building. She waves urgently at me. I join her, and she crouches, pointing in the window. "We have a big problem."

A lace curtain covers the pane, but I can make out several images through it. My stomach drops. "You've got to be kidding me."

Logan and Charles are bound to chairs gathered at a round white table in the back. Trays of cupcakes are everywhere. Partially eaten versions lay in front of them, and crumbs litter the floor. Frosting covers their lips, and their eyes are closed, heads lolling in what appears to be sleep.

"She's poisoned them," Persephone says, making my blood run cold. "They don't have long before they're ghosts, too."

S herlock appears as I consider how and where to break in. The front door is no doubt locked and possibly the rear entrance as well. "Why cupcakes?" he asks.

Persephone and I both spin to look at him. "Go away," she orders. "We have serious business to attend to."

He ignores her and speaks to me. "Ask her."

"I don't really care why she's obsessed with cupcakes," I whisper, furious. An idea hits and I dig in my purse. Since this is still Logan's building, I have a key. Seeing my phone, I text Daddy and ask him to call emergency services and send an ambulance. "She's going down. Now."

Marching up the front steps, I grab the doorknob. The key is out and ready to use, but the handle turns easily in my palm.

I march inside and discover her humming to herself in the work room. The oven is on, filling the redesigned kitchen with heat, and she's wearing another of her aprons. Stacks and stacks of cupcakes cover every surface. There have to be hundreds.

She looks up from frosting one, a bag of blue icing in hand. "There you are. It's about time. We've been waiting for you."

Her ghostly apparitions float nearby, but seem uninterested in me. After our confrontation the previous night, I think the odds are in my favor of taking her down. "I want to help you, Trysta."

"Well, at least you got my name right." She returns to her task. "But you can't help me. What's done is done."

"I can cross them over. The ghosts. They won't bother you anymore."

A dry chuckle leaves her lips. "If they die, I die. If I die, they do. See where I'm going with this, honey?" She glances up. "I don't have a death wish, so..." She shrugs. "All I want is to have a life. Bake cupcakes. Be normal, like you."

"Me?" I laugh. "Poisoning Charles and Logan will land you in prison. You won't be baking anything there."

She tosses the bag down. "I didn't poison them. They're just sleeping. A sugar coma, you might call it." She giggles. "No one can resist my cupcakes, except you, apparently. Besides, I would never hurt Logi."

And I'm Martha Stewart.

A blur of orange catches my eye as Tabby streaks past my feet. She hides behind the trash can in the corner. I left the door open and she must have sensed I was here. "I need the necklace. I can release you from this...whatever it is, but I have to separate you from the spirits."

"Sorry." She fiddles with the apron. "That's not happening. I'm the one who needs the necklace. What did you do with it?"

"Sorry?"

"I know you took it." The airhead expression she prefers to wear leaves her face, making her features hard and unforgiving. "If you don't give it back—"

Sam appears. "Tabby stole it."

Trysta's eyes track him as he hovers at my side. "That cat makes me want to scream," she says.

"Join the club," I mutter, but mentally praise my grandmother for her thievery. "Go check on Logan and Charles," I tell Sam.

He floats through the wall and Trysta cries, "Get back here!"

It's not her voice, but that of another woman. I blink and then see a fuzzy blob of a spirit superimposed over her. It's like a photo from a film camera, where two images are caught simultaneously.

She *is* possessed!

By who, though?

I need my iron cross, and the spell I used on Reverend Stout. "The necklace is at my house," I state, bringing her attention once more to me. "Let's go get it."

She holds out a hand, and the double exposure phenomena happens again. Trysta's voice wavers, the sound of the second mixing with it. "Bring it to me."

If I can get her across the street, the ghostly energy will wane. "If you want it, you have to come with me."

Persephone shoots me a quizzical glance. "What are you up to, spirit walker?"

"We can work out a compromise." I'm glad Trysta can't see or hear her, and I hope Persephone will catch on. "I'll eat a cupcake if you come to my house."

Trysta's lips tighten. "Promise?"

I draw an invisible X on my heart with Logan's key, holding my other hand behind my back with fingers crossed.

Sherlock emerges from the rear. "Ask her."

Trysta looks between us. "Ask me what?"

I trust the ghost, so although I'm anxious to get out of here, I follow his instructions. "Why cupcakes?"

Her demeanor changes and she giggles again. She sounds

like herself now, the second ghost once more taking the back-seat. "They were Mammie's favorites."

Mammie. A term used for grandmother. That's who's inhabiting her body. "Your grandmother, Mabel?"

She smiles and examines the cupcake she's finished frosting. "The lightning strike screwed up her taste buds and her palate went numb. Except for cupcakes. She could taste their sugar and she craved them day and night. Dr. Fred, he ran all kinds of tests and couldn't figure it out. Her parents refused to give her nothing but desserts, though, and she ran away from home a few times. They were awful to her!"

I'm not sure where the story is going, but Sherlock nods and looks satisfied. I feign being shocked. "That's terrible to treat her that way."

"I know, right?" She places the dessert on a tray with a dozen others, all in cotton candy colors. "They finally put her in a home, can you believe it? Said she was cuckoo. Dr. Fred got her out when she turned eighteen and promised her all the cupcakes she could eat if she married him. Isn't that romantic?"

Or creepy. Where is that ambulance? "Sure," I say, playing along.

Sam appears. "The brothers are alive. Weak, I dare say, but alive."

"I told you, silly." Wiping her hands on her apron, Trysta comes around the table and motions me to head for the front of the store. "They'll be fine. Forever in love with me and my confections, but I promise I'll take good care of them. Let's go get my necklace."

Sickness churns my stomach. I walk to the door, her behind me. How am I going to do this? "So Mabel and the doctor married and he ran tests on her, right?"

Trysta picks up a cupcake from the counter. "She ate these all day, every day and he did research on her. They were happy, but eventually, grandma weighed three hundred pounds. Dr. Fred couldn't even move her on his own. He rigged up a chair for her and when they were out during a storm, well...oops."

She makes it sound as though being killed by lightning was no big deal. I glance at the spirit I assume is Dr. Fred. His gray face is bland.

Outside the night air is humid and I'm already sweating. She closes the door after us as I hope my plan to get her inside my place will work. Tiny rocks on the street crunch under my shoes and an owl hoots in the woods past the cul-de-sac. "That's too bad about the doctor."

"Neither of them knew she was pregnant with my mom at the time. Luckily, Arvin came along. He's the one I remember," she continues. "He became my mom's father and took care of her. An odd child, though, like me. She and grandma fought all the time."

We reach the gate and I open it, allowing her to pass through before me. "Families. What can you do?"

She practically skips up the sidewalk to the front. "My mother was embarrassed by her. Ran off to Mexico as soon as she could and that's where I was born."

Perhaps that's why Daddy couldn't find a birth certificate for her.

"When we came back," she continues, "she was working as a waitress and fell in love with Larry. Except she couldn't escape our family history. Lightning loves us."

I think about lightning loving the transformer this week. Maybe I need more than my cross for this. "And Larry paid the price."

"She knew it was her fault. Tried to kill us both in that accident, only I lived. Ended up with Mammie. On her deathbed, she told me the stories my mother had refused to. That's how I learned about our odd history. She also gave me a cupcake. A special one, she called it, like me."

"She's special, all right," one of the gargoyles says. "Cuckoo as the clock inside."

At the door, the shadows are heavy around us and my pulse triple-times it. Persephone and Tabby have followed us at a distance. Sam and Sherlock hang back to keep eyes on Logan and Charles. I pray my plan works. "And you decided to become a baker."

"There's a secret ingredient in them, passed down from that one Mammie gave me. That's why everyone who eats them loves me."

Except for those like Gloria who have a bad reaction. "Wow. It must be something unique."

Her teeth are white in the murkiness, her smile appearing predatory. "She never felt loved, only used. She wanted to make sure I didn't have to go through what she did."

I step across the threshold and flip on the lights. "That was nice of her, but what is it? What's the secret ingredient?"

She follows and heaves a sigh, the attached ghosts staying outside on the porch. "Her," she says. "She gave me a piece of herself that day, so she'd always be with me. And I've been adding a bit to every batch I make."

The implication stops me in my tracks. "A bit of *her*?"

Her chin bobs and her eyes glitter. "Her essence." She holds out the one she's brought along. "You did promise to eat this."

"Don't you want your necklace first?"

She winks. "Once you taste this, you'll do whatever I want."

I take the thing and act like I'm admiring it. "Looks absolutely delicious."

"I blend a drop of my essence, along with hers, into the batter. She taught me the words to say when I mix it in."

Blood magic, only not the kind we'd thought. "Oh." I don't know what else to say, outside of "gross!" I peel off the paper liner and act as if I'm taking a bite, making sure a bit of frosting sticks to my upper lip. I mimic chewing, and nod as though my taste buds love it.

Trysta's features fade slightly, Mabel's taking their place. "Where's the necklace?"

I reach for a tissue and wipe my lip, swallowing hard to make sure she believes I've eaten a bite. I've no idea where Tabby might have placed the jewelry, but the cross is in my bottom desk drawer. "Right this way," I say, hiding the uneaten cupcake in my hand and leading her to my office.

The teddy bear squawks and Trysta flinches. "Sorry," I say, hustling to the bookshelves. It gives me an excuse to buy time, and distract both her and the ghost riding her. I set the cupcake behind a table lamp before I fumble with the switch on the EMF reader. The squawking stops. The camera? I let that run.

Trysta turns toward the display window. "Is that a siren?"

I pretend not to hear it, my relief at the approaching ambulance making my legs weak. "Must be a residual effect from the bear," I tell her. "You know, like when a smoke detector stops and you can still hear it?"

Facing me once more, she seems doubtful but doesn't argue. Her countenance keeps switching between hers and Mabel's. "Well? Where is it?"

At this point, I can't tell who's asking, and it's freaking me out. Tabby and Persephone enter, the cat jumping up on my desktop as the angel looks on. Trysta shrinks away from the feline.

"Why do you need it?" At my desk, I open the bottom drawer, thankful that Tabby is holding her interest by pawing the air and meowing loudly. The cross lies in a box with the written spell for exorcising a ghost from its vessel. I act as though I'm putting my purse inside, grabbing my stun gun first. "It contains your grandmother's secret ingredient, I bet. Her *essence.*" Just saying it makes me squeamish.

The siren grows louder. The spirit of Mabel surfaces. "You nosey troublemaker," she seethes.

Under her grandmother's influence, Trysta reaches for me. "I'll kill them all, including your precious Logi."

"Okay, first of all, it's LOGAN." Right before she grips my neck, I flip on the weapon and zap her.

Her body goes rigid, grimace frozen in place. Stiff as a mannequin, it teeters and then topples over, disconnecting from Mabel and her ghosts.

The grandmother howls and flies at me. Snatching up the cross, I raise it like a shield and stand my ground. "Secondly, it's time you crossed over, Mabel!"

The iron works, repelling her. She's thrown backward, Trysta still lying on the floor, unable to move.

Mabel is undaunted, however, and tries to attack again. I grab the paper with the spell on it, as the ambulance screeches up outside and the siren ceases. As I say the words, I step over Trysta and march toward her grandmother. Realizing the gig is up for good this time, Mabel's eyes widen with fright, and she waves her hands at me, begging me to stop.

I'm almost finished reciting the words when a fist hits my lower back. I grunt, knees buckling, and find Trysta has regained control of her body.

Staggering, she rushes me, and we go down in a pile.

The front door flies open. "Ava?" Daddy yells.

I bring the cross down on the back of her head with all my might. She hollers and rolls off.

Mabel hovers over me. "I will kill you," she snarls.

"Go to the light," I huff, as Daddy grabs my arm and helps me to my feet.

Mabel cries out, and Trysta lies on the floor, rolling around and holding the back of her head. The spirits of Dr. Fred, Arvin, and Larry are still outside. As I recite the spell, Mabel rages and tries to stop me, but she's now unable to reconnect to Trysta, who is disconnected from the others. Without her vessel, Mabel has no anchor.

Before I finish the last line, she blinks and flickers out.

"Did it work?" Daddy asks, looking down at Trysta. "She's still here."

"She's not a ghost, after all," I tell him, and check for signs of Mabel. I see and hear none. "Only possessed by one, and that individual seems to be gone."

He gets me to my chair and hauls Trysta up. Jones walks in. "This her?" he asks Daddy.

My father confirms it is.

"I have video of her attacking me," I tell Jones and point to the bear.

He looks at the stuffed animal dubiously, then shakes his head. "A shame. I liked her cupcakes." He takes Trysta's wrists and brings them behind her. "Trysta Harding, aka Stacey Bollinger, you are under arrest for identity theft, assault and battery, attempted murder, and whatever else I can come up with once I've figured out what all you've been up to."

"No, wait." She turns puppy dog eyes on me. "Tell him, honey. I would never hurt anyone. It was Mammie. She made me do all this."

Jones looks around, suspicious. "Who's Mammie?"

"Mabel Bollinger," I tell him. "Her dead grandmother. She's gone now."

"Huh." He steers Trysta toward the door. "So a psyche eval is in order."

She argues with him every step, her eyes shooting daggers at me. "This is all *her* fault! Ava is who you should arrest!"

"Trust me, I would if I could," Jones drawls.

As they go out, Jenn and Lia rush in. "What happened?" Lia asks, her eyes behind her glasses as big as saucers. "We heard the call on the police scanner and got here as fast as we could."

"Long story," I tell them.

"Does this mean I should cancel the Country Club reservation?" Jenn asks.

"Yes." And boy, am I relieved. "The party is off." I face Daddy. "Is Logan okay?"

He offers me a hand. "Let's go see."

TWENTY-FOUR

I have visited the hospital far too many times this week.

Logan and Charles have their stomachs pumped, and I hedge about what type of poison Trysta used to the doctor, who asks about it. Detective Jones interviews me, too.

"I don't know what it is," I tell them both. This isn't entirely a lie. "All I know is what she told me—it makes some folks crave her cupcakes, and others get sick from it."

"A drug?" Dr. Ernestine, the on-call physician, glances at Jones. Her brow is deeply furrowed and her eyes tired. "Must be a potent one."

"We'll test the food. Then we'll know." Jones says.

"Whatever it is, it pretty much put those two"—she points toward Intensive Care, where the brothers share a room—"in a light coma. I've had six other folks from Thornhollow in here this week, either vomiting their guts up or in a similar state."

Six. Gloria was only the tip of the frosted iceberg. I feel lightheaded and lean against the wall.

"You look a bit weak, yourself." She watches me over the

top of her reading glasses. "Why don't we step into that empty room over there so I can examine you?"

"I'm fine. Are your other patients okay?"

"Yes," she says, pointing past the admissions desk at an elderly man wheeling a woman to the main exit. "There goes the last of them now. She was in a full-blown coma state for days, and I couldn't figure out why, but now I know. She ate that gal's cupcakes. It was the only common denominator for all of them, but until tonight, I didn't think anything about it."

The man pushing her is the one from the elevator. He looks happy and relieved. "Could you excuse me?" I ask. "I know them."

I don't wait for an answer and walk quickly to the gentleman's side, fighting my dizziness and upset stomach. "Do you remember me? From the elevator the other day?"

He stops and scans my face. "Irises!" He snaps a finger. "Of course. Is your friend better?"

"She is, and it looks like your wife is, too."

The woman glances up as I move so she can see me. "I remember you," she says.

"I think you're confused," her husband gently chastises. "I met her in the elevator the other day. She had a flower arrangement with your favorites in it. That's how we got to talking."

She smiles and winks at me. "Oh, right. Sorry, you looked familiar."

It's clear she's humoring him and recalls her out-of-body experience. "I'm so glad you're awake and going home."

"Me, too. Guess something I ate didn't agree with me."

"I heard it might have been a cupcake. Was it from the new bakery?"

"It's not open yet, is it?" her husband asks.

She fiddles with her sleeve. "There was a lady handing out pretty pink and blue ones in front of the grocery store

Sunday afternoon with some grand opening flyers. I stopped after church for vanilla. I'm a baker, too, and I needed some for my cookies. She was so lovely and she was giving away those pretty samples. The one I had sure was delicious."

"Did you take any home with you?"

"No. Why?"

At least there's no danger of her eating another. "Just wondering." I step back. "I should let you go. I bet you're more than ready to be home."

We say our goodbyes and I return to the ICU. Jones is writing in his notepad. Dr. Ernestine is speaking to a nurse at the crescent shaped station in the center of the hub. Through the glass of the room, I see Logan stir. "Can I go to him now?" I call to her.

The doctor comes over to me. "Your friend, Gloria, told me about what you do."

My already touchy stomach jolts. "Event planning, yes. Do you have something you'd like help with?"

"Not that." She rubs her eyes under her spectacles. "The other thing. With"—she looks around and lowers her voice—"you know."

Here we go. "Do you have a problem?"

"The morgue does."

That's no surprise. Persephone appears behind her. "This could be a tough one, spirit walker."

Goodie. "I imagine that's not uncommon."

The doctor rights her glasses. "Can you help?"

"I have other things on my plate at the moment."

She checks her watch, as if realizing she does, too. "Soon. Can I come see you? Explain what's been happening?"

Diving into my bag, I find a business card. "Call me."

She examines it and slides it into her lab coat pocket. Her

head inclines toward Logan's room. "Fifteen minutes. He's very weak."

Before I can get by him, Jones raises a finger to stop me. "Off the record?"

I just want to see Logan, but... "What can I help you with?"

He mimics the doctor, glancing around to make sure no one is close by. "Was there a ghost forcing her to poison people?"

"There was. Mabel was using Trysta to stay earthbound, and that included drawing energy from the living. I believe she intended to plug herself into the whole town through the cupcakes."

He screws up his face. "For what purpose?"

I think of Sam wanting to be a living human being again. "Mabel may have believed she could draw enough from others to become corporeal once more."

Skepticism is evident in his tone. "Through cupcakes."

I dig out the necklace Tabby left in the drawer. Examining the contents of each pendant revealed nail clippings, hair, and yep, someone's blood. Probably Mabel's. "I know this isn't what you want to hear, but I think the 'poison' was blood magic." I hand him the piece of jewelry. "Mabel gave this to her granddaughter and I'm betting the organic material inside those lockets are used with a spell."

He cringes but accepts it and doesn't attempt to refute my theory. I decide to call that a win. "The lab techs aren't going to find any actual poison in these or the cupcakes, are they?"

"I don't know what they'll find. I'm sorry I can't be of more help."

He cocks his chin toward the room. "Go see Logan. We'll talk again about all of this."

"I can hardly wait."

He snorts and I leave him.

Logan is awake and reaches a hand for me when I enter the

room. I take it and he pulls me to him. His strength is returning quickly and I'm relieved. "Are you all right?" he asks.

"Me?" I chuckle. "You're the guy in the hospital bed."

"You look pale."

"I'm fine, buster, and I explicitly told you not to eat the cupcakes."

He chuckles. "She forced me, I swear. Told me she'd kill Charles if I didn't."

Helen sweeps into the room, a nurse on her heels insisting that only one visitor at a time is allowed. She vanquishes the young woman with a practiced hairy eyeball that has sent many folks cowering. "What on earth have you done to my boys?"

"Mother!" Logan rubs a hand over his face. "Will you stop? Ava saved us."

"It was Trysta, Mom." Charles is awake, too. His head is turned away from us. Shame coats his words. "I knew there was something weird going on, but I didn't know what. I got to the point where all I could think about were those cupcakes. Morning, noon, and night, I wanted those things. Craved them like an addiction. I couldn't stop, and when I asked her about it, she laughed it off and said they were magic. I...I love her, but..."

After all this? I'm floored.

Helen frowns and goes to his side. He wipes at his eyes and I realize he remains under Trysta's spell, regardless of the spirit connection being broken. "Why didn't you say something?" Helen asks.

"I didn't know how." He keeps his gaze on his blanket. "Admit it, it sounds ridiculous."

"You're not the only person it affected," I tell him. "Trysta was putting something odd into her batter. Whatever it was, it caused most people to crave them, and several suffered from various degrees of unconsciousness after eating one."

Helen meets my eyes. Her voice is indignant. "She drugged my sons? I'll have her roasted on a spit!"

"Mother." Logan sounds beyond frustrated. He points toward his brother, and softens his tone. "Charles still *loves* her."

She sees her other son is fighting tears and places a hand on his arm. "I'm sorry. I cared for the girl, too, but this is an outrage."

Logan squeezes my hand. "Tell us what happened. All of it. They deserve to know what you found out about her."

While Helen already knows a few details, I relate the rest. Shocked silence meets my claims. It's a lot to take in.

Charles shakes his head. "She had spirits attached to her, and she was possessed by her grandmother?"

I nod. "The lightning strikes did a number on both Mabel and Trysta. It's as if they both had some kind of internal antenna that attracts that type of phenomena. Their experiences caused them to be able to see and hear the spirit world because they technically died and then came back. It also seems to have given them unnatural abilities to manipulate energy, at least in the form of human beings. We are all energy, first and foremost. Trysta may not have realized Mabel was using her to juice her up enough to return to physical form, but regardless, their plan to drug our entire town in order to make people love those cupcakes, and in turn, Trysta, was extremely dangerous. And you, Charles, could have ended up in a permanent coma."

He and Helen are speechless for a minute. Then she clears her throat. "It appears we owe you our gratitude," she says.

Logan looks relieved. He entwines his fingers with mine. "Thank you for saving us."

His sibling sits up and faces him. "Can you help her, Logan? She's going to need a good attorney."

Helen rounds on him. "Are you out of your mind? She tried to kill you."

"She didn't mean it." He pins me with a hopeful gaze. "Right, Ava? It was her grandmother calling the shots."

"I'm *not* representing her," Logan tells him.

The doctor enters, a thundercloud above her. "These are my patients and your time is up."

Helen argues, but Logan swings his legs out of the bed and motions at me to grab his clothes. While the doctor and mother argue, I help him dress and we sneak out, both women's protests following us.

At home, we curl up together on the couch and fall into a deep sleep.

TWENTY-FIVE

I wake Saturday morning to find a host of people, living and dead, crowded into my house.

Not to mention Moxley and the cats enjoying all the attention.

Helen is staring down at Logan and I, giving us both a start. We sit up hastily, and I eye the fancy dress she's wearing. "You have my blessing to do the handfasting ceremony," she says.

"The what?" Logan asks, running a hand through his hair.

"Handfasting." Sage enters and yanks me off the couch, my body groaning in protest. She's also dressed more formally than I'm used to seeing, gliding around in a deep purple chiffon. "It's a Celtic ritual where the hands are tied, symbolizing the combining of two lives. Think of it as a compromise. Today, you get to do a short, sweet ritual in the backyard."

"And come October," Helen adds, "you marry properly."

"I'd like to rent the bakery space," Sage announces. "I want to open a tea house."

The segue leaves all of us with our mouths open.

"Okay?" she asks, with a hint of impatience.

"Uh, sure," Logan says. "I guess that would be fine."

"It's not like Trysta will be using it." Sage glances toward the front windows, her face full of contemplation. "The pastels have to go, but it's already set up for baking, so I can have tea blends and desserts. A few witchy things, too. Tarot cards, crystals, dried herbs, you know, the usual."

I'm still aghast. "What about your sisters and the Emporium?"

Her focus returns to us. "Raven did a reading and it was spelled out in the cards. I'm supposed to take a new path. I can still help them if they really need me, but being here in Thornhollow is my destiny."

The way she winks at me when she says it tells me more than her words. Her destiny is to help *me*. "It will be great to have you right across the street."

"I've said for years we need a tea house," Helen adds before smiling and leaving us.

That settled, Logan and I are swept up by friends and family. I'm led upstairs by Gloria and find my dress waiting for me. She seems restored to her good health, and my gown is no longer in pieces. She helps me into it and Brax does my hair and makeup—nothing fancy, but I do feel glamorous when I return downstairs.

"I appreciate what you did for my sons," Helen tells me as we peer out the kitchen window while folks gather on the lawn.

Rhys and Charles chat with Logan near the gazebo. Moxley is at Logan's feet, taking it all in. Logan is dressed in a charcoal suit that sets off his eyes, and Charles looks better, although his normally buoyant spirit is subdued. "Did you initiate this?" I ask.

Her lips purse. "I took your advice, in a way."

Arthur and Lancelot check their dishes to see if there's

food. Since there isn't, they leave. Brax assured me upstairs that Rhys had already fed them. "You did?"

"I never had a chance to ask Logan what he wanted, but I didn't need to." She keeps her focus on him and Charles. "You make him happy, and he wants you to be the same."

The gazebo is being decorated by Betty, Mama, and Queenie with loads of flowers, both from Aunt Willa's garden and Betty's flower shop. Daddy and Logan's father converse down by the homestead, examining the ongoing work, and Brax and Rhys call them closer to pin boutonnières on their jackets.

I've been instructed not to show myself until the wedding march begins. "I promise to do everything in my power to keep that smile on his face," I tell her as I watch Logan laughing with my dad. "And I'm sorry about Trysta."

Helen sighs. "What are we going to do with all those cupcakes? After confiscating a few, Detective Jones has released the crime scene."

"Keep Charles away from them," I suggest. "I believe the connection is broken, but we should burn them to be on the safe side."

"A bonfire it is. I'll take care of it." She faces me and gives me the once over. "You look lovely."

"I'm so glad you're here."

This lands me a smile. "Me, too. We still have to discuss the ghosts at the vineyard."

"I can come for a visit next week."

"I would like that."

She leaves and Persephone pops in next to me. She's wearing all white, even her jewelry, and resembles an angel without wings. "What a nice day."

I'm filled with joy, hope, and optimism. My dream is coming true, and we even have Helen's blessing. Talking about ghosts isn't what I want to do, but I need to know something. "Did Mabel cross?"

"She did, as did the male spirits attached to her and Trysta."

"Will Trysta be all right without her?"

"I believe she's already seen a specialist and been labeled with mild schizophrenia. Some medication and a stint in an appropriate hospital for six months for evaluation has been ordered."

"She won't be charged with a crime?"

"Yes, but I believe the extenuating circumstances may reduce her sentence. Time served in the mental institution may be an option. There is the identity theft and attack on you, if you press charges."

I'm relieved. "Charles is still in love with her. Best if I don't."

"Romantic, isn't it?" She winks when I grimace at her mimicking Trysta's previous words. "But enough about them. It goes against the rules, but I'm telling you anyway. Trysta and Charles will work out in the end. There, happy?"

My jaw falls open. I'm not sure how I feel about that.

Sherlock appears next to her. "I am."

She glares at him. "What are you doing here?"

"Sam and Tabitha invited me."

At that moment, my shapeshifting grandmother enters, fully human and dressed in one of my designs. Gloria accompanies her, looking proud. "What do you think?" Gloria asks. "Fits her perfectly, doesn't it? It's like magic."

It sure is. "You are stunning," I say.

She mocks a bow. "You keep insisting I wear clothes, and I happen to enjoy this frock. I shall wear it whenever I can."

My heart warms. Sam joins us and has a similar reaction to

mine. His eyes bug out and his mouth hangs open. "My dear, you are extraordinary."

My grandmother is stealing my limelight, but I don't care. "Who's going to perform the ceremony?" I ask. "I know Aunt Willa did a few, but I'm not familiar with handfasting."

"About that," Persephone grins. "I called on our old friend to help us out."

"My old…" Understanding dawns. "Winter's here?"

As if on cue, she strolls in wearing a blue dress with rhinestones that flash in the light. Her crazy curls are tamed in a sophisticated updo, the silver strand left trailing down onto her shoulder. "It's not your design," she says, "but I hope it's acceptable."

I throw my arms around her and squeal. "I can't believe it!"

"I wouldn't miss this, and I'm ordained to do the ceremony. All we need is the official marriage license."

My smile falters. "Oh no! I don't have one."

Persephone points out the window. "He does."

Reverend Stout and his wife have arrived and are chatting with Helen. He has his Bible and a sheet of paper. I breathe a sigh of relief. "Well, then, what are we waiting for?"

Sam takes Tabby's hand and kisses it. "Perhaps we should renew our vows."

She sidles up to him and circles his phantom waist with her arms. "And then indulge in another honeymoon."

They kiss and we all turn away. I notice Sherlock and Persephone giving each other a long, heated glance. "Please make peace with each other," I tell them. "You're so good together, and you both deserve to be as happy as I am right now."

My angel lifts her nose. "I'll think about it."

She whisks through the back door. Sherlock winks at me

before he darts after her. "I promise to make you a very happy angel," he calls.

"I wish Rosie could be here," I say, more to myself than anyone else.

"I think Sage has that covered," Winter tells me, pointing out the window. "See that chair up front with the computer tablet on it? She's got Rosie on a video call from the hospital so she and the baby can watch."

It's all so perfect. Jenn, her sister, Penn, and Lia join the group. Bis does too, finding Sage and hugging her. Even Baylor, the librarian, turns up.

Music begins to play from the outdoor speakers. Rhys lines up the men and Brax seats Betty, before taking his own spot in the gazebo.

Daddy rushes in. "Hello," he says to Winter, before he turns to me. "My goodness, Ava. You look amazing."

I tear up. "Oh, Daddy. I can't believe this is actually happening."

He hugs me and pats my back. "No crying, now," he says gently. "You'll ruin your makeup."

Winter takes her place on the stage. Logan, Moxley, and Charles stand to one side, Brax on the other. He's been my best friend since we were kids, and is acting as my man of honor today.

The wedding march begins and Daddy and I step from the back porch into the sunlight. Across the yard, Logan's smile nearly brings me to tears again. As all eyes land on me, I return it, knowing this is just the beginning.

Those in the chairs stand, and Mama and Queenie both dab at their eyes as Daddy and I proceed down the steps and onto the carpet runner. All the way to the structure, my gaze is on the man I'm about to marry.

Sunlight streams into the open dais, bouncing off his hair.

The scent of roses and jasmine dances in the air, birds singing along with the music. Daddy hands me off with a kiss to my cheek and Logan and I take our place in front of Winter.

As the music fades, Logan leans close and whispers, "You are drop-dead gorgeous."

I don't know how, but my smile grows. "You're not so bad yourself."

"Greetings, friends and relatives," Winter says. "Today, on this momentous June fourth, we gather in Miss Willa's lovely garden to witness her niece, Avalon Fantome, and Logan Cross, bind their lives together. In so doing, they create the union of their hopes and desires, now and in the future. They vow to be partners, through the trials and triumphs of their shared life, which have already been many." She winks at us. "They declare to each other and to all of us present that they will be by each other's side, no matter what life brings their way."

Logan envelopes my hand with his. "I don't have a ring," he says in my ear.

I let myself get lost in the feel of his strength. "We don't need any."

Winter continues. "Ava and Logan, love brings all of us together today, and should be the basis of everything you do going forward. To love and be loved unconditionally is the greatest gift of all. As the two of you stand here before these witnesses, I ask you this: will you honor and respect each other always?"

"We will," we say in unison.

"Will you share each other's pain and sorrow, as well as each other's joy?"

Logan's palm is warm and steady in mine. "We will," we chorus again, our voices intertwining like our fingers.

Willow takes a white satin ribbon from around her neck. "Present your hands, please."

We lift our joined hands and she lays the strip of material across them. "This represents the bond you forge here today. Are you willing to make this commitment for now as well as forever?"

Logan turns to stare into my face. "You bet your life I do."

"Ditto," I say. "Now and forever."

Winter begins to wrap our hands. "Like this ribbon, your love is strong enough to hold you together, yet flexible enough to encourage personal growth and individuality."

A cool breeze ripples across my shoulders. A fresh wave of jasmine teases my nose. "This is perfect," I hear Aunt Willa say. "Exactly what I fantasized for you."

I can't hold back the tears any longer. Winter has heard her, too, and winks at me. "As your hands are bound together," she says, winding the satin around our wrists, "I ask you to declare your intentions for each other and this marriage."

Logan clears his throat. "I, Logan, take you, Ava, as my friend and wife. To love and respect, support and hold you, to make you laugh and to be there when you cry. I will be your companion and your best friend on this journey that we now take together."

He's so elegant. Me, not so much. "I, Ava, take you, Logan, as my best friend, husband, and partner." I take a deep breath. "I've known you my whole life and I can't imagine it without you. What we have is like nothing I've ever experienced, and I'm beyond words to explain it. All I know is that you've saved me in more ways than I can count, and there's no one I'll ever share a deeper connection to than you. In this life, and the after. Plus," I add with a grin, "you don't think I'm bonkers since I see ghosts."

That garners chuckles from the crowd. Logan laughs as well.

Winter forms a knot. "As your hands are now bound

together, so shall your lives be bound as one. Let this ribbon act as a reminder of your promise to one another, and let no one unbind it as long as you both shall live."

We skip the ring exchange, and Reverend Stout joins Winter and places his hand over ours. "By the authority vested in me by the State of Georgia," he says, "I now pronounce you husband and wife."

"Can I kiss her now?" Logan asks.

Winter nods. "Go in peace. Live in joy."

As my husband wraps his unbound arm around me and brings his lips to mine, those gathered send up a cheer. Mosley barks and I hear Aunt Willa say, "May you always be this happy."

I will, I promise her and myself.

Logan breaks the kiss. "I love you, Ava."

My heart melts. "I love you, Logan."

The sun shines warmly on us as we turn and greet our audience. I see Persephone and Sherlock near the roses holding hands, Sam and Tabitha, too. When I glance at the porch, I even see Aunt Willa. She blows me a kiss and I give a start when I see the ghost girl from Hannah's plantation with her. Another female spirit stands slightly behind the girl, a hand on her shoulder. The resemblance is obvious—it's her mother. She gives me a deep nod of gratitude. My efforts must have helped the girl's spirit pass to the other side to join her family. I acknowledge them all and they fade away, the young girl giving me a bashful wave before disappearing.

"Thank you," I say to everyone as we accept congratulations from the crowd. Going back down the aisle, Mama and Daddy are the first to greet us. "I know you've got better things to do tonight," Daddy says after hugging me and shaking Logan's hand, "but if you want to see your old man perform at the benefit, I've reserved seats for you."

Logan's father steps across the aisle. "Helen and I would like to come as well, if that's all right with y'all."

Helen looks less than excited, but Daddy lights up. "Why, that would be great."

The others gather around and I garner many hugs and kisses, even from my mother-in-law. More folks ask if they can attend Daddy's show and his delight makes me happy all over again. He declares he'll have a whole section waiting for us.

"Looks like we'll have a caravan heading to the hotel," Brax announces. "Let's meet at the B&B at six, so we have plenty of time to get through traffic."

Everyone agrees. Logan whispers in my ear, "I'm up for it, if you are."

I grin and nod. "We'll be there, too," I tell Daddy.

Then I tug on the ribbon and lead my husband inside to start our new life together.

STAY TUNED **for more adventures with Ava, Tabby, Logan, and the rest! Tea Leaves & Troubled Spirits, coming Fall 2022!**

READY FOR MORE MAGICK?

Don't miss the next exciting adventure! Sign up for Nyx's Cozy Clues Mystery Newsletter.

And check out these magical stories!

Sister Witches Of Raven Falls Mystery Series

Of Potions and Portents
Of Curses and Charms
Of Stars and Spells
Of Spirits and Superstition

Confessions of a Closet Medium Cozy Mystery Series

Pumpkins & Poltergeists
Magic & Mistletoe
Hearts & Haunts
Vows & Vengeance

Cupcakes & Corpses

Once Upon a Witch Cozy Mystery Series
If the Cursed Shoe Fits (Cinder)
Beastly Book of Spells (Belle)
Poisoned Apple Potion (Snow) - only available in the Black Cat
Crossing box set which is FREE when you sign up for the
Whiskered Mysteries newsletter!
Red Hot Wolfie (Ruby)
Hexed Hair Day (Rapunzel)

ABOUT THE AUTHOR

USA Today Bestselling Author Nyx Halliwell is a writer from the South who grew up on TV shows like Buffy the Vampire Slayer and Charmed. She loves writing magical stories as much as she loves baking and crafting. She believes cats really can talk, but don't tell her three rescue puppies that.

She enjoys binge-watching mystery shows with her hubby and reading all types of stories involving magic and animals.

Connect with Nyx today and see pictures of her pets, be the first to know about new books and sales, and find out when Godfrey, the talking cat, has a new blog post! Receive a FREE copy of the Whitethorne Book of Spells and Recipes by signing up for her newsletter http://eepurl.com/gwKHB9

CONNECT WITH NYX TODAY!

Website: nyxhalliwell.com

Email: nyxhalliwellauthor@gmail.com
Bookbub https://www.bookbub.com/profile/nyx-halliwell
Amazon amazon.com/author/nyxhalliwell
Facebook: https://www.facebook.com/NyxHalliwellAuthor/

Sign up for Nyx's Cozy Clues Mystery Newsletter and be the FIRST to learn about new releases, sales, behind-the-scenes trivia about the book characters, pictures of Nyx's pets, and links to insightful and often hilarious *From the Cauldron With Godfrey blog*!

DEAR FABULOUS READER

I hope you enjoyed this story! If you did, and would be so kind, would you leave a review on Goodreads, Bookbub, or your favorite book retailer? I would REALLY appreciate it!

A review lets hundreds, if not thousands, of potential readers know what you enjoyed about the book, and helps them make wise buying choices. It's the best word-of-mouth around.

The review doesn't have to be anything long! Pretend you're sharing the story with a friend. Pick out one or more characters, scenes, or dialogue that made you smile, laugh, or warmed your heart, and tell them about it. Just a few sentences is perfect!

Blessed be,

Nyx 🤍

www.ingramcontent.com/pod-product-compliance
Lightning Source LLC
Chambersburg PA
CBHW070946190726
48292CB00004B/1349